'That's nonsense. I love Craig—*and* I trust him.'

Blaine lifted his glass in mock toast. 'And I admire your touching blind trust. Too bad he's not here to witness it.'

Every stool in the small bar, off the restaurant, was occupied now, as more people arrived for lunch. Syrie and Blaine were crushed together, so that their knees were touching. She felt the warmth of his and was aware of the masculine and disturbingly familiar scent of him.

DIAMONDS
AND DAISIES

BY

WYNNE MAY

MILLS & BOON LIMITED
ETON HOUSE   18-24 PARADISE ROAD
RICHMOND   SURREY   TW9 1SR

First published in Great Britain 1989
by Mills & Boon Limited

© Wynne May 1989

Australian copyright 1989
Philippine copyright 1989
This edition 1989

ISBN 0 263 76345 5

Set in Plantin 11 on 11 pt.
01 – 8907 – 53550

Typeset in Great Britain by JCL Graphics, Bristol

Made and Printed in Great Britain

CHAPTER ONE

THE JET airliner prepared for touchdown and Syrie Knight's green eyes, widely spaced and fringed by dark lashes, searched for a glimpse of the Indian Ocean island and then she saw it—thinly veiled peaks, coral-fringed, white-foamed bays, exotic palm trees and, of course, that incredible sapphire, turquoise and jade sea. Cane fields came rushing up to meet the plane, and the landing-gear dropped into position. The wheels bumped and tyres screeched before they caught and held on the tarmac. No matter how many times she had flown, this was always her tense moment, where every muscle in her body seemed to lock.

Immediately the aircraft came to a standstill, passengers began reaching for flight bags and attaché cases and then prepared to disembark and, finally, to cross the tarmac.

Busy and colourful, Plaisance Airport came up to Syrie's expectations. Feeling excited now, she managed to get through passport and health control in a short time, and then her eyes searched for Craig Knox.

There was no sign of him and, taking a chance that she would not miss him when he did turn up, she went into a bank and cashed a traveller's cheque. There was still no sign of Craig when she came out of the bank, and she pushed her trolley towards a seat and sat down to wait for him.

Mauritius might be an emerald, palm-fringed dot in a limitless ocean, but the airport was as busy as many of the international airports she knew. Jets, after all, flew in and out of Mauritius from Africa, Europe, Asia, Australia and the neighbouring islands of Réunion, Madagascar and the Seychelles. When they'd met and fallen in love in Greece, Craig had told her that air passenger traffic between the islands of Réunion and Mauritius alone was fairly heavy.

Wearing navy trousers and a pleated bomber jacket in pure linen navy and white houndstooth checks, with a plain white crêpe de Chine blouse which had a floaty white tie, she felt that the warm air seemed to cling to her and, feeling restless, she stood up and began to push her trolley in the direction of the entrance terminal building. At this rate, she thought crossly, she'd get to know Plaisance Airport pretty well. In Athens, Craig had explained, over a small table with a cloth the colour of a Medici green emerald, that Plaisance, surrounded by cane fields, meant The Place of Pleasure, but at the moment she wasn't feeling much pleasure, and the irritation she had been coping with was beginning to give way to a niggling worry.

After several more minutes, she looked in on the bar restaurant, but there was no sign of Craig. Taxis, she discovered thankfully, seemed to meet every plane. Jokingly, Craig had said that the taxis on the island were the cheapest in the world, but often ancient and rattling.

Glancing at her watch again, she decided to phone the studio, and delved into her Florentine leather bag for her notebook. After finding the number, she began to dial. There were long moments before the receiver was picked up at the other end.

'Design Dimension. Good day.' The male voice was deeply pitched and the accent attractive.

Keeping an eye on her luggage on the trolley, she said, 'May I speak to Craig, please?'

'Craig is away at the moment. Can I be of any assistance?'

Syrie was shocked, but in control. 'Did he say where he was going?'

'Right now, he's on a shoot in Réunion.' The voice was also slightly impatient, and she could imagine him picking up a sheet of paper so that he could scan through what was written or typed on it while he talked to her.

Feeling slightly disorientated at this piece of news, she brushed a strand of tawny hair—which curled inwards around her neck—from her face. 'A *shoot?*'

'In other words, he's taking photographs.'

'Oh, a shoot! Of course. How stupid of me.' She took a ruffled breath. 'But, you said Réunion. I—I—just don't get this. To whom am I—is this . . .?'

'This is Blaine Cartwright. Now, what can I do for you?'

Craig had told her all about his partner, Blaine.

'By the way—you must be wondering—I'm Syrie. You know—Syrie Knight. *From Athens*. I'm speaking from Plaisance, of course.' She laughed a little. 'Craig was supposed to have met me but, quite obviously . . .'

Blaine Cartwright's interruption was brutal and to the point. 'Quite obviously he's forgotten.'

'Well, thank you.' Syrie's voice was like ice. 'Thanks for cheering me up.'

'Look,' she knew Blaine Cartwright would be glancing impatiently at his watch, 'I'll come for you. Give me twenty minutes or so.'

She gave way to sheer irritation. 'Please don't worry. I can hear you're busy. I'll take a taxi.'

'Don't get on your high horse, Syrie Knight. I said I'd pick you up. I'll be there.' She felt sure he'd just lifted his lashes to reveal impatient—what colour?—eyes.

'I'm not getting on my high horse. That is just where you're wrong.'

He went on, 'I know you're put out, and what's more, I don't blame you. Craig's an idiot. He often forgets things like dates and what time it is, but apart from that we're pretty busy here, right now. That's why he's in Réunion, after all.'

Syrie gave the mouthpiece the benefit of a frustrated stare.

'When will he be back from Réunion?'

'Your guess is as good as mine, actually. OK, I'll be seeing you . . .'

'When I said I'd take a taxi, I was thinking of you, *actually*.' Her fingers went to her hair again.

'Oh, well, that's nice—but let *me* think about me.' Before she could say anything else he had rung off and, replacing the receiver, she went in search of a seat where she could try to feel cool and could scan new arrivals at the terminal entrance.

The airport had just emptied itself for the third time when she saw him, and what was so crazy was the fact that she felt instant excitement. With almost mesmerised fascination, she watched Blaine Cartwright striding over to where she was standing.

Tall and lean, he moved with a casual masculine grace. His oatmeal linen jacket, carelessly held by one finger, was slung over his shoulder. His body—his well-exercised body, she thought—seemed to ripple easily beneath his clothing. He had an island tan, of course, which drew immediate attention to his blue eyes and his dark blond hair. At the moment he was frowning, and she had the feeling that, should the occasion arise, he could be hard and ruthless and even downright selfish if he wanted something badly enough.

Those blue eyes came as a positive shock. Holding her gaze with his, a tantalising groove appeared in one cheek, although he had not actually smiled.

'Was I long?' His eyes then looked her over, and she was fully aware of the blatant interest in them. Unaware of anything but the moment in question, she was overwhelmed to find Craig's partner such a 'turn-on'.

She managed to laugh—quite lightly, she thought. 'No. Actually, you were very quick. I had just been on another grand tour of Plaisance. I feel I know it backwards by now, I might add.'

She was tall, but he was taller than she was and his blue eyes absorbed her own.

'Were the grand tours to keep you from screaming with frustration?' He went on looking at her, as though his thoughts were not actually on what he was saying, and she found this disconcerting.

'Well, yes. Let's face it, I *am* surprised at *this* turn of events. I just can't understand how Craig could have forgotten the date of my arrival . . . how he couldn't have arranged for someone else to go on this shoot.'

'Me—for instance?' The groove in the cheek came into play, mocking her.

She lifted one shoulder. 'Well . . .'

'Talking about the date of your arrival, Syrie Knight, let's just call it the *fate* of your arrival, and be done with it.' Their eyes met.

'Fate has nothing to do with it.' Her smile was deliberately wide. 'I'm not sure I understand you.'

He took his time answering. 'Somehow, I think you do, but in any case, I want you for myself—now that I've seen you.'

'You're kidding.' She hadn't bargained for this lot.

'Not in the slightest.'

After a moment she made herself think. 'Well, that's your problem. Besides, don't *I* come into this?' Her voice had a cutting edge now. She wished he didn't have this power to fluster, excite and even depress her.

He regarded her with a speculative expression.

'You know the answer to that as well as I do.' He tossed his jacket over one of her bags.

She still had her hands on her trolley. 'I am beginning to think that you're exceedingly tactless, Blaine Cartwright,' she said, beginning to move away from him.

She drew a little breath as he reached over and took the trolley from her, his hands brushing hers. His, she was quick to notice, were tanned and infinitely masculine.

He began to lead the way to where his car was parked, and she watched him a few moments later as he shrugged himself into his light jacket and then stacked her luggage away.

When they were in the car he turned to look at her, and the space between them was suddenly charged with something like an electrical current.

'So, you're from Athens?' He sounded almost amused about this.

'Yes.'

'A place, as I remember it, of white-hot afternoons and shuttered streets; nights filled with the throb of bouzouki music; ouzo and retsina wine and, of course, the rumbustious Greeks themselves—except that it was our Craig Knox who appeared to have knocked you *temporarily* off your feet.'

A gust of rage swept over her. 'Not temporarily. We have to be very clear about that.'

He made no attempt to start the car. 'That remains to be seen, but tell me, what were you doing living in Athens when you are so obviously "frightfully British"?'

'What do you think I was doing? I was working there.' To conceal the tension she was feeling, she went on casually, 'How are things at Design Dimension, by the way?' She knew the studio operated from Blaine's large colonial-style house.

He started the car and began to reverse from the parking space, touching her shoulder—deliberately, no doubt—with his own, as he turned to glance in the direction of the rear window.

'We're getting it together. Everything gets done. It just takes time and a lot of hard work.'

Glancing at him, she saw that his chin was firm and his lips—well . . . pure sensuality. She took a ruffled little breath. Why are you letting this guy get at you like this? she asked herself.

They were both silent for a while, and then he turned to her again, and for a wild, frantic moment she wondered if he'd seen the cane truck surging towards them, hugging the centre of the road and going like a bat out of hell—but he had. Even at this early stage, she was becoming horrified by the driving techniques, which seemed to involve a lot of hooter blowing. Without even realising it, she released a long, pent-up breath and she heard Blaine's soft laugh.

'Well, did you get a huge fright, Syrie from captivating Athens?'

'Yes, I did actually.'

'You'll get used to it.' His smile was slow and aggravating.

'Will I?'

'Uh-huh. Believe me. It becomes a kind of survival beat in the end.'

'I see. Thank you for putting me wise.'

Her clothes, which had been so right for an expensive luncheon party in Paris, where she'd boarded her plane, were beginning to stick to her back, and she found herself longing for a bath in frothy, perfumed water.

In an almost theatrical voice she said, 'I'm feeling terribly hot and sticky. There was no time to change into something more comfortable before boarding the plane at Charles de Gaulle airport. You see, I'd been in Paris to pick up my wedding dress, which had to be altered slightly, and then I'd been to a farewell lunch with some *ver-ry* smart people. The survival beat is different there.'

'I'm sure. And now, with your wedding dress carefully folded in whispering tissue-paper and reposing in one of those expensive, brand new bags, you are becoming increasingly aware of those intangible doubts which have begun to work their way into your mind. Right?'

In a soft voice she began to sing, ' "Listen to the mock-ing bird. Listen to the mock-ing bird." I don't need this, Blaine.'

'In other words, you're feeling a little out of sync, Syrie—now that you've met me.' He laughed, just as softly.

Angrily, she said, 'I just don't believe I'm having

this conversation.'

'But you are, and you know why.'

'I don't know what gave you that idea. If I *am* beginning to have doubts, they're about *you*. I'm not sure Craig has the right kind of partner.'

'No? Maybe, Syrie, I should just remind you that Craig was only recently offered a partnership in *my* business. Maybe I'm beginning to ask myself the same thing.'

'Really?' She was really steamed up now. 'I'm sure Craig would be knocked out to know the truth. Anyway, it might have been a whirlwind romance—well, I suppose it was—but I have no doubts.'

'Famous last words,' he replied easily. 'By the way, before I left home I gave Liselle instructions to prepare a room for you. Liselle is my housekeeper. There's no point in going to Craig's chalet, after all.'

Syrie felt confused and angry at the same time.

'I would prefer to go to Craig's chalet—that is, of course, if I can get into the place. The problem here is I seem to remember Craig saying he has a maid who leaves about two every day.'

Looking back, she remembered Craig saying— 'Every day, my maid prepares a meal for me, before she leaves about two. You know the sort of thing—a casserole, cold cuts and a salad in a wooden bowl. Sometimes I eat what she prepares and sometimes I don't. It just depends.'

Before Blaine could answer, she went on, 'Would you mind taking me there first? Maybe the maid leaves later some days.' She strove to keep her voice calm. 'Honestly, I'm trying not to have prehistoric views about all this, but Craig could have remembered the date. He'll probably feel like kicking himself when he finds out what's happened.'

'I'm sure he will.' Blaine's voice was heavy with sarcasm. 'I don't blame you for feeling hostile, though.'

'Well, I'm nursing a very personal grievance, after all.' Her voice was suddenly furious—the way she felt.

'Especially when you know what is involved here.' His smile was full of meaning.

Her reaction was immediate. 'I'm afraid I don't get this. What is involved? What are you going on about?'

'I'm talking about us, but I guess you knew that all along, without having to ask.'

She took a loud breath. 'You keep referring to us. You know, as if we were a couple of larger-than-life soap-opera characters who have just come face to face with the sudden and completely shattering knowledge that they have fallen instantly in love, when they have no right to, since another person—*maybe persons?*—is involved. And what is this reference to famous last words? I'm totally in love with Craig.'

'Don't overlook one thing. Most soap operas—I would even go so far as to say *all* soap operas—have a twist in the ending.' He turned to look at her with those exciting blue eyes.

'And some man is always in devious pursuit of some woman who does not—and never will—belong to him. So just make up your mind to that, and I'm not talking about soap opera. I'm talking about us. I have no wish for you to create misunderstandings. You might enjoy being considered excitingly dangerous and sexually aggressive, and all that jazz, but try to understand that I have no intention of becoming involved with you—or anybody else, for that matter.'

He maddened her by saying, 'You are involved and

you know it. These things happen, and forget about
the soap opera.'

Suddenly, she thought it best to laugh. 'Oh, come.
This absurd conversation has gone on long enough,
don't you think?'

'What shall we talk about? The weather?' he asked.

'Yes. I was going to ask about the weather, actually.
I'm dreading the cyclone season, by the way.'

He laughed. 'Oh . . . like in Athens, we have our
shutters. A lot of things go on behind those shutters
during a cyclone, believe me.'

She drew an impatient breath and turned her face
away.

'I find I don't want to talk,' she said. 'Not even
about the weather. Do you mind?'

'No, but only because we've reached Craig's chalet.'
he answered carelessly.

He stopped the car and switched off the engine, and
then he leaned over and opened the door on her side.
She could hear his breathing and she was aware that
he had used Aramis cologne, probably after he had
shaved that morning.

'I might as well warn you,' he was saying as he drew
back, 'that Craig's phone is mostly out of order.'

'Well, since I don't intend using the phone at this
particular time, it won't make any difference to me,
but thanks for the warning, anyway.' She lifted her
elegant long legs and then stepped from the car.

As Blaine saw to her luggage he said, 'This chalet
used to be "shot". Craig had it made over into what
you see now.'

Syrie's eyes had noticed the new windows and front
door. At the end of a paved path there was a white-
painted wall, with open squares in it, and a fancy
white-painted archway.

'He told me about the alterations,' she answered. 'Apparently they involved a lot of hard work.'

'And expense.' Blaine spoke with something like contempt in his voice.

Syrie felt another surge of rage. 'That, I imagine, is Craig's business.'

'And I would like to *think* of it that way, believe me,' Blaine answered, as he began to lead the way towards the archway. 'In case you're interested, Syrie,' she heard him say, 'the chalet was built in 1904.'

'Nothing interests me right now, just as long as there happens to be a nice, veined marble bath.'

'There is a bath, of course, and it's a wonder it *isn't* marble, but maybe he couldn't find one expensive enough. Craig likes only the best.'

'I don't think that's very funny,' she snapped.

Ignoring her, he went on, and she realised that he was doing his best to infuriate her. 'But . . . if it's any consolation, there's a very nice splash pool in the patio area, along with a pergola trailing jade vine. What's more, the pool is surrounded by large peach-coloured tiles. If you go ahead and marry this guy, you'll be able to sit there and think about what a huge mistake you've made.'

'In other words, I should marry you?' Suddenly, she began to laugh.

She watched him go towards a potted plant. 'There's a chance the key might just be in here. I've seen Craig go to it. Ah, you're in luck—if you can call it luck.' He inserted the key into the lock and stood back, after he had opened the door.

'Since you know the way about, you go first,' Syrie said. Her green eyes were still glittering and clashed with his. 'And maybe you'll give me a break now.

OK? I've been wondering what makes you tick, actually. This—ah—teasing—is it a sickness over which you have no control?'

He gave her an easy smile. 'There's nothing sick about me, and I'm always in control. Well, I guess it's up to me to show you around and get you settled, unless we just call it a day and head right back to my place?' His eyes were mocking now.

'We'll call it a day and I'll stay right here, while you head right back to your place.'

'Says she, already regretting her decision.'

Syrie said nothing.

Her eyes immediately went to work. Craig had told her about the restored Morris chairs and his collection of big posters, which he had bought while in London and Paris at one stage in his life. She took an instant dislike to the wooden settee, which had cushions stacked against the back, but, making up for the settee, there were two plumply upholstered chairs and a sofa to match, in colours which corresponded with the peach-coloured tiles and the water in the splash pool, since the pool was tiled in blue. At the end of the living-room there were big glass doors, and Blaine folded them right back, creating one large space, which was more cheering. Potted plants stood about on the tiles, and there was a short palm tree, which had an abundance of brilliant green leaves.

'Since I happened to sleep in the guest-room one hectic, boozy night when I attended one of Craig's parties, I know where it is,' Blaine was saying. 'I'll take your things through.'

'That's fine. I guess he's had it prepared for me, anyway.'

'Are you hungry?' Blaine asked.

'No.'

'Thirsty?'

'Yes, but water will do.'

The room was plain, with a *dhurrie* rug. White-painted cyclone shutters were closed, creating a gloomy coolness. There was a big bed with a dark fuchsia-shaded bedspread, and the covers on the pillows were navy with fuchsia dots. Several Mauritian baskets were scattered about, and there was a pot plant and white bookshelves. One of Craig's posters, depicting a play which had been running while he'd been in London, had been mounted and fixed into position above the bed.

'I guess I'm also suffering from thirst right now but no water, if I can help it. I'll see what I can get together, Syrie.' She felt the full force of Blaine's stunning blue gaze.

'Thank you. Something other than water *would* be nice, after all.' She tried to inject a little enthusiasm into her voice, since he had been good enough to leave his work at the studio to rescue her.

At the door, he turned. 'By the way, I hope the bath comes up to expectations. I can't really remember.'

'It was an idiotic thing to have said. I didn't expect a marble bath.' Her voice had an edge.

When she joined him in the living-room a few moments later, she was quick to notice that he had poured himself a Scotch. Glancing at his watch he said, 'I've decided to call it a day by pouring myself a stiff Scotch.'

'Why? Have I been such a strain?' She smiled, but it was all surface.

'It has been quite a strain.' A groove appeared in his cheek. 'I feel—well—concussed. You know—knocked on the head—bowled over.'

'Why don't you go and pour me a drink?' she said in a snappy voice.

'What would you like? I find that I can mix you a Scotch or a very potent island cocktail.'

'A very potent island cocktail. Flying, combined with meeting capricious characters, always makes me feel jaded. Besides, it is getting on for good old sundowner time, I should imagine.'

While he went to mix her cocktail in Craig's kitchen, Syrie walked out to the splash pool area and, after gazing down at it for a moment or two, she went to sit on one of the wooden folding chairs, which were draped with deep-blue canvas.

Blaine returned and passed her a tall glass. Smiling down at her, he said, 'I've been hunting around in the kitchen for something to go with a cocktail—a cherry, an olive . . . or something. All I could find for your very exotic—*otherwise*—cocktail was mandarin.'

She laughed, but there was a brooding expression in her green eyes. 'Oh, gosh, you didn't have to go to all that trouble, Blaine. Anyway, I've always loved mandarin—when I could get it.' She lifted the glass to her lips; careful not to dislodge the section of fruit which he had draped over the rim. '*Yassou* as they say in captivating Athens, Blaine, and thank you for bringing me here all in one piece. I was beginning to wonder. I couldn't get over the driving I saw today.'

'Not mine, I hope?'

'No, not yours.'

'You'll get used to it, as I said.' He toasted her good health. '*A votre santé*, Syrie, as we say in the Jewel of the Indian Ocean.'

As he went to sit down, she said, 'By the way, the bath's OK.'

He moved his shoulders. 'Good. A bathroom

equipped with a sophisticated bath is, after all, one of life's pleasures.'

She took a sip of her cocktail. 'Mmm . . . I can see what you mean by potent.'

'Don't you like it?'

'I like it very much. That is what's worrying me.' There was a silence and then she went on. 'You must be very busy for Craig to have forgotten the date of my arrival. For all that, I must admit I'm feeling very let-down.'

'We are busy, but Craig has always been bad with dates and with the time. Maybe he'll change, now that you're here. Maybe he'll even get around to thinking about you twenty-four hours a day.' The way in which he said this infuriated her.

'I don't expect any man to think of me twenty-four hours a day. Credit me with some integrity.'

'Let's get back to your whirlwind romance of the year.' His arrogance took her breath away, but she willed herself to keep quiet, while he went on, 'You are shortly going to make the discovery how little you know about Craig Knox. However, now for the good news—*but* for that mistake, you wouldn't be here.'

'And we wouldn't have met. Is that what you're trying to say?'

'That is exactly what I *am* saying.'

He had all the arrogance of a jungle cat, she thought, and trying to hold on to her temper she said, 'I know enough about Craig Knox. Don't permit it to worry you.'

Blaine took a swallow of his Scotch and went on looking at her for a moment. 'And so, believing this, you threw all caution to the winds in Athens? Maybe behind some of those shutters?'

'No, I didn't throw caution to the winds. Not that

it's any of your business.'

'Why was this? Craig's not usually so slow.'

'For one thing, I had absolutely no intention of landing up at some private wailing wall in Athens, after he had returned to Mauritius and had decided, maybe, that marriage was just not what he had in mind, after all.' She made a gesture of annoyance. 'Just let's stop this.'

'In other words, you didn't trust him—in that case?' He looked at her through thick lashes and she got up impatiently and went to stand next to the splash pool. She regained control and, laughing a little, she swung round.

'You know, I'm wrestling with myself whether or not to throw something at you.' She glanced around and her eyes came to rest on a large ceramic elephant.

'Throw it, if you wish, but it would appear that I am beginning to get through to you.'

'Get through to me—*what*?'

'Craig has let you down, just by not being here, right this minute. He will go on letting you down. Make up your mind for it, before it's too late. How did you meet him, anyway?'

'Why should I tell you?' She gave a little shrug.

'If only to make me jealous, maybe.'

'I met him at a roof-wetting party, as it so happens.' She turned her green gaze on him.

'But you'd gone there with someone else, of course?' His smile was no more than a deepening of the groove in his cheek.

'Yes. I'd gone with someone else, after passing through kilometre after kilometre of one jumbled town after another: half-finished buildings and thick-trunked trees, which had been whitewashed round the middle and which were topped by round green bunches of foliage. You've been to Greece. You should know the set-up.'

'I know the kind of towns you're talking about —where men sit together on shop verandas, or beneath trees, perched almost on the end of their seats and yet appearing utterly relaxed.' His sudden smile was devastating, almost thrilling her to the soles of her feet.

'I see you know,' she laughed. 'Tell me, though, have you any idea what all those half-finished buildings, small junk yards, lumps of concrete, tiles, bits of machinery and bags of goodness-knows -what are all about in the midst of pink oleander, cypress and olive trees?'

'Sure. A Greek starts to build for his family in slow stages. First, he purchases the bricks, then the tiles and so on. All—bit by bit, and then he finally begins to build the house. And so, you were in on a roof-wetting party?'

'Yes. After having travelled for most of the afternoon. Eventually we reached this place. The heat was stupefying. Remind me about it, whenever you hear me grumbling about the heat in Mauritius—I've heard Port Louis can be hot. In fact, it was so hot that when I was introduced to Craig, he said, "I don't know where the Greeks get the energy to compose such lively music. They must compose it all in the winter." '

Blaine seemed to uncoil himself from the low chair. 'And so, you found him very amusing? What else did he have to say for himself on this memorable occasion?'

'Try not to be so sarcastic. Anyway, I'll tell you. He said that it was plain to see I had been expensively educated and that I was beautiful and cared for.'

Blaine put his glass down and then shrugged himself out of his light jacket and tossed it over the back of a chair. 'You've just reminded me that it's hot and that I need another drink. Give me your glass, Syrie.'

'I shouldn't,' she murmured. 'I'm feeling quite . . .'

'Good.' He took the glass from her and disappeared in the direction of the kitchen, and when he returned he handed her a fresh cocktail.

'What happened to the other piece of mandarin?' He sounded amused.

'I ate it. It was delicious. I told you I like mandarin.'

'Well, I've given you another piece. I threw the worm away.' He grinned down at her, and she thought how tanned and sexy he looked.

She lifted the fruit from the rim of her glass, using her perfect oval nails, and popped it into her mouth.

'I'll eat it now.' When she had, she smiled at him. 'Tell me, were you on holiday in Greece, or was it a business trip?'

'I was on holiday, with a bit of business thrown in.' He swirled the contents of his glass and she heard the rattle of ice-cubes.

'When was that?' Her green eyes searched his face.

He lifted one shoulder. 'Let's see : . . two years ago, almost to the date.'

'Gosh, *I* was there then.'

'It would have saved a lot of trouble if we'd met there.'

'I wouldn't put it like that.' Her voice was full of taunting amusement. 'Tell me, was there a girl? In Athens?'

'Since you ask, yes. Her name was Tonia. She'd been to university in Athens and she made an excellent guide. We parted very good friends.'

'And of course she must have been beautiful?'

'She was. Like you, she had gorgeous, golden-brown skin.'

'What else?' She was surprised that she was disconcerted by all this.

'She had dark, shiny hair. Shoulder-length. She was

wearing—are you still interested?' His voice was mocking.

'Yes, of course.'

'She was wearing something like a toga. White cotton. Very like one of those ancient Roman citizen's flowing garments, usually with a purple border. Hers was trimmed with lace and threaded with gold cord, and it offered her a freedom of movement which was wonderful to watch.'

'What a wonderful memory you have.' She did not try to keep the bite from her voice.

'Well, naturally, when it comes to something like this. Her toga—what-have-you—came down to her sexy, sandal-strapped ankles. Super.' He took a long breath.

Unreasonably niggled, she said, 'Although you have mentioned that you parted good friends, you sound as if you were completely "thrown" by this girl, Tonia—was it?'

'You'd give anything to know, wouldn't you?'

'How did you meet this gorgeous creature?'

'I hired her to take me to the Acropolis. Ah, I remember it well.'

With a sense of shock, Syrie realised that she was jealous.

'Weren't you capable of taking yourself off to the Acropolis?'

'Of course. I'd already been there; once by myself and later with a group. For obvious reasons, I decided to hire Tonia privately to take me there again. I wanted to get to know her.'

'Did she realise you'd been there before?' Syrie swung one foot and looked down at it.

'What do *you* think?' He glanced at his watch. 'To get back to the present, though, what are your plans?'

'My plans?' Her laugh was brittle. 'I had no idea I had

a choice—with Craig away. I'll just have to sit around and wait for him to turn up.'

'Well, I've already told you—Liselle has prepared a room for you.'

'Thank you, but I'll stay here.' She realised how flat her voice sounded.

'Before I go, I'll check the phone,' he said.

'There's no need to check the phone. I guess I'm quite capable of working out whether it's in order or not.'

He ignored her sarcasm. 'I'll come back later. We'll go out to dinner.'

She felt embarrassed and furious. 'I'll be fine. All I want is a cup of tea and maybe a snack. There must be something I can rustle up.'

As he reached for his jacket he said, 'You didn't get round to telling me what you did in Athens.'

Her anger towards Craig was getting in the way, and she found herself snapping. 'What difference does it make what I did? I was in nuclear physics.'

She could see that she had angered him.

'Did that make you feel good?'

'I'm sorry. Unlike you, I don't usually rely on cheap sarcasm. It's just that, at this moment, Athens seems a long way off. So does the roof-wetting party, for that matter.'

'Forget about Athens and the roof-wetting party, Syrie.'

'*Why?*' Her voice was aggressive.

'Because there's no point in brooding about it.' Their eyes locked for a moment. 'The fact that Craig has had a place in your life is inconsequential now.'

'You seem to have a talent for saying vile things, Blaine. Anyway, thanks for the lift from the airport. I'll see you to the door. Don't bother to come back. I'd rather not go to dinner.'

'You'll feel differently later on,' he answered.
'I wouldn't bet on that.' She waited for him to leave.

CHAPTER TWO

AFTER Blaine had gone, the chalet seemed very quiet. Syrie went through to the bathroom to prepare for a bath. It seemed a hundred years since she had boarded that plane at Charles de Gaulle Airport. Quite suddenly, she felt tired of travelling about; tired of working in one city after another—since the untimely death of her beloved parents in England—but she'd felt the need to travel and to keep on moving to ease the awful pain and loss. She'd had to struggle with upgrading her French when she'd worked in Paris, and she'd done her best to learn Dutch and Italian. She found herself thinking of the friends she had left behind—Pierre in Paris, which city, for her, had revolved around fashion and perfume, since she had landed herself in a position as buyer for Chez Michi. For a while, she had thought she was in love with Pierre, who had wanted to marry her. He had gone to some length to stress that his mother, under whose thumb he appeared to be, would expect him to marry in the Madeleine Church and to go on living in her apartment.

In Holland, she'd found a position which entailed some office work, along with showing diamond rings, mostly to tourists. In Holland, there had been Hans who, like her, was not interested in falling in love and settling down.

With considerable apprehension she later moved to the tawny city of Rome. Ah, *Roma*, she thought now, as she padded about Craig's chalet in her bare feet. It had not taken her long to find work in an art gallery and, when in Rome, she had 'done the lot'. In Rome, of course, there had been a man in her life, but nothing serious; a handsome Roman, and with him she had visited the museums and churches, not to mention the Vatican and the Catacombs—those subterranean cemeteries which had given her claustrophobia, much to his concern. She had dined and danced at all the popular Roman nightspots. Her thoughts brooded on her tiny apartment in a restored building in Rome. It had been furnished and, to her amazement, two magnificent oil paintings graced the living-room. There had been a small garden at the back, with the usual pink, white and red oleander bushes and an 'umbrella pine'.

Before she ran her bath, she looked into a cupboard and found freshly laundered towels, and within a few minutes she was stretched back in the deliciously warm water, which she had expertly bubbled and perfumed.

For a long while she lay with her eyes closed, and then she sat up and soaped herself. It was only then that she really noticed the white daisies, in a basket, on the vanity unit. Somehow, the arrangement did not seem to go with the rest of Craig's chalet, but then he *did* have a maid who had probably arranged the flowers. Standing up, she reached for a large towel and wrapped it around herself.

She washed her hair and went back to the bedroom to look out her small hairdryer and a container of L'Oréal Free Style mousse. Going back to the mirror in the bathroom, she was surprised to see another container of the same mousse, which was behind the glass sliding doors of the wall cabinet. Then her eyes went to the tiny diamond-stud ear-rings which appeared to have been carelessly dropped next to the mousse.

Staring at these feminine items, Syrie went rigid. I don't want to live like that, she thought; not ever knowing if Craig is being unfaithful or not.

After she had styled her hair, shaping it inwards, she unpacked a few clothes and hung them up. She looked out a pair of white trousers and a golden-yellow shirt, over which she intended wearing a chunky gold belt with an ornate clasp. With her thoughts festering elsewhere, she applied make-up.

Her romance with Craig, ending in Athens when she had driven him to the airport in her car, had been brief, and she realised now how little she knew about him. In a stark moment, she asked herself whether she had, indeed—according to Blaine Cartwright—courted disaster, from the moment she had agreed to become engaged to Craig, in Athens, with the understanding that she would join him in Mauritius, where they would be married.

On the day they had chosen her engagement ring, they had had a light lunch, and Craig had seemed on top of the world. That night, they had dined high up and overlooking the glittering lights and traffic of Athens, while a young man played hits from the Beatles on a grand piano.

'This always strikes me as comical,' she'd said to Craig. 'I've listened to someone playing Noël Coward in London, which is appropriate. You'd think this guy would play Greek music, wouldn't you?'

Obviously madly in love with her, Craig was instantly jealous. 'And so, this is one of your dining-out haunts?'

'Well, yes. It's very popular, after all.' She kept quiet about Stavros.

'With someone special?'

'Craig,' she'd answered, quite honestly, 'there has been no one that special in my life—ever. Up until now, of course. You're special.'

'Am I?' His eyes had narrowed.

'Of course. Why am I wearing this?' She held out her hand.

'And yet you won't let me near you. This is something I can't understand. When two people are in love, they show it, right?'

It was true. Although she had been tempted to make love with Craig, she'd held back . . . just as she'd always done with the others.

Craig's phone, she discovered, was indeed out of order. Feeling totally depressed and fed up, she made some tea which she drank next to the splash pool. She did not feel like eating. Not yet, anyway. Maybe she would make some toast later. She had noticed some salami in the refrigerator.

Later, and acting on an impulse, she went to stand just in the doorway of what was, obviously, Craig's bedroom. Her eyes flickered around the room. A number of brass Indian bangles were scattered about the top of a chest of drawers, but she realised that Craig was one of those collectors with no particular collection in mind. The bangles could have, quite simply, appealed to him.

The maid, on the other hand, could have arranged the daisies and removed her ear-rings while she was cleaning the bath. At a push, the mousse could belong to Craig.

When she heard a car pulling up outside, every muscle in her body seemed to tighten up. Blaine must have arrived to take her to dinner. Why couldn't he have listened to her? She was filled with humiliation and her helplessness at the situation in which she found herself;

before anger took over.

She almost ran back to the patio and, since she had left the front door open, she sat down and pretended to be looking at a magazine when he walked in. His car keys dangled from his fingers.

'I tried to ring you.' She saw impatience on his face. 'His phone is out of order again, right?'

She gave a little shrug. 'I particularly asked you not to come back, Blaine.'

Ignoring her, he went on, 'I couldn't get through to Craig in Réunion. Get some things together, Syrie. You're coming back with me.'

'Why couldn't you get through?' she asked.

'For the simple reason that he was not in the hotel. I'll try again later, if it will please you.'

'Please don't worry. I'm not.' She looked at her nails.

In one movement, almost, Blaine had reached down and pulled her up towards him, drawing her up along the length of his body. Before he released her, he said, 'Don't be so stubborn. Besides, your eyes say yes.'

'You don't have to worry about me. I'll be quite safe here.'

'You'll be quite safe with me, too. Haven't I told you—I have a nice, old-fashioned housekeeper?'

Syrie found herself laughing. 'Who just happens to retire round about seven-thirty, right? I'm used to that one, believe me.'

'While you're getting your things together, I'll close up here—and don't argue, Miss Knight.'

Blaine's colonial-style house stood on a bluff, and then the ground sloped down to where a flagstone path and steps led to a curved stretch of beach. The sun had set, but Syrie's eyes feasted on the mass of tangled pink bougainvillaea, pink frangipani, hibiscus shrubs with blooms of pink, crimson, yellow and white, which were lit up by tall white garden lamps. Leaning palms were also intensified by the garden lamps and, despite being so near to the beach, the lawns looked as smooth as green velvet. A light breeze blew in from the sea and the waves could be heard as they crashed down on the coral reef.

A downstairs veranda, with elaborate white lattice-work, was topped by an identical upstairs veranda, and both ran the length of the house and then extended to one side of it, on the ground level. All the French doors had beautiful fanlights.

Craig had explained all this to her in Greece, and so she knew about the downstairs veranda on the side of the house, which had been glass-enclosed to accommodate Design Dimension. There was, he had explained, another room which led off the area and was occupied by the commercial artists employed by the studio.

Blaine reached over and opened her door, and she felt his warm breath on her bare arms before he drew back. She stepped out, feeling the cool breeze on her face.

She was about to reach into the back of the car for her flight handbag when Blaine said, from behind, 'I'll see to that, Syrie.' He brushed her skin with own and she automatically drew an unsettled breath and moved quickly to one side. He had, she'd noticed at the chalet, changed into white denim trousers, a navy loose-knit shirt, white casual shoes and socks, and he looked absolutely 'heart-throb-ish'.

As they walked towards the house he was saying, 'As you have probably judged for yourself, this property enjoys the most spectacular daylight views, but then, it's been here a long time and one of my ancestors had an eye to business, when he sailed to Mauritius and built this house. Eventually, my grandfather owned it and, in turn, my father inherited it. I was next on the list, but after my mother died my father decided that I should become the owner and enjoy the house. He was perfectly happy with a suite of rooms, which is very private, but he remarried recently, and has gone to live in her chalet, which is very nice and suits their life-style.'

The doors to the entrance hall were open to reveal an exciting space of classic black and white marble flooring, upon which stood several pieces of antique furniture, and a winding staircase. To the left was the drawing-room, and to the right, the dining-room.

Syrie looked up at the glittering chandelier.

'This is just what I always imagined a big plantation house to be. It is like a *Gone With The Wind* house, isn't it?'

'Well, in its day it used to be a sugar plantation house. As a matter of fact it has a history span of over a hundred and fifty years. The sugar plantation itself dated back to 1740 The sugar planters produced poor quality cane.' He crossed over to a gleaming bureau and opened a drawer. 'Actually, there is a reference in this diary to the effect that the sugar was only fit for mixing with plaster as a form of protective cement. This was used to coat the fascias of houses.'

'Oh, what a waste!' She widened her green eyes.

'One day, you might like to have a look at the diary. It's quite interesting.'

'I'd like that.'

'On a more cheerful note,' he went on, smiling at her, 'the planters soon learned and so, what happened? We had the sugar barons and they made a lot of nice money. This, in turn, allowed them to live in paradisal style. Actually, a lot of treasures, like this furniture you see here, were brought to Mauritius by these sugar barons. Years later, the land was cut up and sold and, as you have seen for yourself, no cane.'

'They must have grown sugar almost down to the

sea—since the house is so close to the beach.'

'Yes, they did. I'll tell you more about it later, if you like. In the meantime, I'll show you to your room and you can settle in. When you're ready—we'll have a drink before dinner,' he said, as they went up the stairs. 'By the way, the room Liselle has prepared for you is not often used but, like the rest of the house, it is always kept aired. I hope you will like it.'

'You're being very kind to me, Blaine.' She kept her voice cool.

'You'll discover, Syrie, that when I'm being very kind I'm normally being very selfish.'

'I see. Well, yes, I can believe that, actually.'

With dusky-pink walls providing a dramatic backdrop to a black French four-poster, the room was absolutely stunning. Standing on either side of an oval, skirted table, two plump chairs were upholstered in black-glazed chintz densely patterned with dark and light pink roses and green leaves. The skirt of the table was made from the same material. French doors and a background of small white-paned windows provided the perfect foil for dark pink velvet curtains. Rose-shaded lamps had been turned on, and the room was filled with the scent of picked roses.

Turning to Blaine, Syrie drew a breath. 'It's lovely. Stunning, in fact.'

'I'm glad you like it.' He smiled easily. 'Although many of the rooms in the house have been changed, this room has remained like this for years. The curtains are pretty faded.'

'Oh, but they look perfect that way.' There was an awkward silence and then she went on, 'You seem to have done nothing else but show me around today. First Craig's chalet, and now this gorgeous house. If—if—one had to describe a room like this, it would probably sound fussy and overdone. Actually you have to *see* it.'

'Well, I've been seeing this room since I was so high.' Blaine extended a hand.

Without thinking, she asked, 'Have you ever slept in it?'

'No, I haven't, but I intend to, since it will be used as the master suite.' His eyes met hers. 'By the way, the bathroom—revamped, in brackets—is through there. OK, Syrie, I'll see you in a few minutes.'

Decorated in soft pinks, the interleading bathroom was also softly lit, and came as a surprise with its large corner spa and a shower stall, behind glass sliding doors. A long double-basin vanity unit ran along the other side of the room, and each basin was served by a large oval mirror in an oyster-coloured frame. There were even two hairdryers fitted next to the mirrors.

After she had combed her hair and scrutinised her make-up in one of the mirrors, she went downstairs and found her way to the drawing-room, where soft coral walls and ceiling beams were the order of the day. Luxuriously comfortable sofas and chairs, upholstered in a rich oyster tone, were banked with coral, crimson and green cushions. The ivory-lacquered coffee-table was huge, and beautiful lamps had been turned on.

'In this house, I don't know where to look first,' she said to Blaine. 'It's all so lovely—what I've seen of it. Are you thinking of marrying soon?'

He laughed at that, and she went on quickly, 'Craig mentioned a nurse.'

'Well, yes, there is a nurse, but Hélène will be going to Réunion shortly, where she will be doing midwifery. Now, what would you like to drink, Syrie?'

'Something deliciously cold and non-alcoholic. Do you have that?'

'I do have that. There's a little bar area, nothing special and converted from a wide passage, actually.'

As Blaine spoke she was aware of the powerful undercurrent between them, even while she stood there, hurting and angry over Craig; smiling.

The bar, as Blaine had explained, was small and cheerful with stools and a long comfortable sofa. A copper jug, holding dried dusky-pink bougainvillaea, stood against a face-brick wall.

Going behind the counter, he began reaching for long glasses, and Syrie did not take her green gaze off him. When he looked up suddenly, catching her, she said quickly, 'I was just looking at that arrangement of dried bougainvillaea. It looks stunning against that wall.'

He glanced carelessly in the direction of the dried and still brightly coloured bracts, which almost concealed the flowers.

'Oh, yes. It was used as a prop in the studio. Liselle probably brought it through.'

Syrie went on making conversation. 'What was the prop in aid of?'

He came from behind the counter and handed her a tall, frosted glass. 'We did a brochure on a new line of swimsuits. This was one of the colours, and so we had some bougainvillaea dried for the set. Liselle is very good at this sort of thing, as a matter of fact.'

Moving with a fluid, masculine elegance, he went back for his own drink and she thought she had never seen such striking, dark-fringed blue eyes. He was wonderful to watch. As though he felt her interested gaze, he turned to look at her and his blue eyes burned back at her.

'So?' He smiled faintly.

'I'm sorry. Did I appear to be staring?' She felt flustered and silly.

'Yes.'

She took a chance on his seeing through her.

'I was thinking, actually. Staring into space.'

'Ah, so you do think? Sometimes?'

They had both remained standing, and he reached for his glass, which was still on the counter.

A flicker of rage went through her. 'I'm not sure how to take that remark, but I think I'm being insulted.'

'I wonder how much thought you gave to rushing out here to marry Craig—and I'm not just staring into space, by the way. You hardly know him.'

'How can you possibly make such a sweeping statement? You don't know how well I know him.'

Leisurely, Blaine leaned his elbow on the counter. 'Let's face it,' his voice had lost its former lightness, 'you got carried away there in Greece.'

'Well, of course I did. I fell in love.'

'Are you telling me that you found yourselves drowning in each other's needs?' He explored her mouth, her eyes and her throat with his stunning blue eyes.

She held the tall glass between cupped hands.

'The way you talk—you don't seem to think much of your partner, do you? Why, in that case, did you approach him about joining your business?'

After a moment he said quietly, 'This is something I've been asking myself recently, as it so happens.'

She hated asking this. 'Is all this to do with his work?'

Blaine shrugged. 'No. Craig is good at his work.'

'So?' Her green eyes betrayed her anger. 'What are you on about?'

'In a nutshell, Syrie, Craig—I have found—is quixotic and artificial. He has lofty, impracticable ideals and, what is more, boasts about them, particularly in the hotel pub. Some of the remarks he has let slip, after he has had too much to drink, make me wonder.'

'I'm not sure I want to go on with this conversation, after all.' She went to the sofa and sat down.

There was a long silence and she crossed her legs. She realised that, when he thought she wasn't looking, Blaine was studying her.

Her thoughts flitted from one unsettling subject to another. Since his own phone was out of order, she reasoned, Craig might have taken the trouble to call her here. Surely, by now, he must have made the staggering discovery that he had forgotten the date of her arrival. If so, he might have made some pretence of caring about not having met her plane and phoned Blaine's house from the neighbouring island.

She was the one to speak first. 'Well, Mr Cartwright, this hasn't exactly been the best day of my life, believe me. If you set out to unsettle me, you haven't exactly failed.'

'My advice to you, Syrie, is—think before you leap into this marriage,' he said bluntly.

'I must point out, Blaine, that I don't need your advice. I'll manage my own life while I am on this island. Look, don't tell me any more. I think this is all I can handle for one day.'

At that moment, plump and homely Liselle came to announce dinner, and Syrie's nerves began to jangle while Blaine made the necessary introductions, causing Liselle to raise her brows, since Craig was not present.

The dining-room was very formal. The table setting was rich with the gleam of polished silver and sparkling crystal. Still beautiful, hand-painted wall murals, which obviously had been done many years ago, provided a softly scenic backdrop for the Chippendale table and chairs. The chairs were upholstered with crimson silk, and at the white-paned windows and french doors bottle-green curtains were tied back with the same crimson material. There were candles on the long table, although a chandelier glittered overhead. Crimson lilies and white lacy flowers had been used to create a dramatic centrepiece. It was like being in another world. All this, Syrie found herself thinking, for two people.

The candles were lit, Blaine dimmed the chandelier and Liselle served the first course—and it was apparent that the dinner service was rimmed with gold.

After Liselle had left, Syrie broke a roll with long, slender fingers. 'Tell me, do you dine in such style every night?'

He smiled, and her eyes brooded on that devilish groove in his cheek. 'How did you guess? Unless there happens to be a dinner party, or when Hélène or my father and his wife are here, I use the breakfast-room. Mostly, I sit on the veranda.'

'And so you don't carry on the tradition of your ancestors?'

They both laughed, and although her mind was consumed by the way in which he had unsettled her, she decided to be pleasant.

'Craig told me about your share in a private sugar plantation on another part of the island.'

'He did? Well, yes, my father wanted to feel free at this time of his life to "do his own thing", and so he made certain decisions. In other words, that I should enjoy this house and the challenge of his various investments.'

She responded with interest. 'You don't seem spoilt by all this.'

'Come, Syrie. I'm thirty. I guess I can handle these things.' He gave her a long look, and she watched him with moody eyes as he poured more pale gold wine into crystal glasses. She picked up her glass, her fingers curling round the long stem.

'The kind of work you do sounds exciting.'

He laughed at that. 'It depends what you call exciting.

It's the kind of work I like, anyway. Recently we were commissioned to do an audio-visual on Chinatown by night. That was exciting—you know the sort of set-up: the gambling shops, restaurants, the temples and the dragon-dance. We took Hélène along. She just happened to be on leave.'

'Up until a little while ago, I was beginning to wonder about Hélène.' Deliberately, her eyes met his.

'Oh? What were you wondering?'

'I was beginning to wonder whether there was some kind of trouble in paradise, and you were taking this out on *me*.' She gave him an innocent look.

'I hope the thought excited you?' He lifted his glass to his lips, and his blue eyes regarded her over the rim. 'Did it?'

'What would you like me to say? That I was excited beyond anything I've ever known? I'm sure, one day, you'll make a wonderful script-writer for a soap opera.' She had decided to sound flippant.

After that, conversation revolved around Design Dimension, and then, dinner over, she said, 'I'm terribly tired, Blaine. I'd very much like to go to my own room. I've brought a novel which I'd like to finish—but I can't even see that happening.

'Is there anything Liselle can do for you?' He sounded suddenly concerned.

'No, thank you. I enjoyed my dinner very much and I'd like to thank you again for everything.'

When they were in the big hall, there was a very tense silence, and then he said, 'So, what now, Syrie Knight?'

She felt a burning resentment.

'I'm beginning to know you well enough by now to know when you're baiting me. Goodnight, Blaine.'

CHAPTER THREE

SYRIE was awakened by Liselle bringing her breakfast on a tray which was brightened with pink and crimson hibiscus flowers arranged in a shallow black vase, and she immediately felt flustered.

Sitting up, she said, 'Oh, good morning, Liselle. How kind of you. I didn't expect breakfast in bed. This *is* a surprise.'

'It is a pleasure, *mademoiselle*.'

'What is the time, by the way?'

'It is eight-thirty, *mademoiselle*. No problem.'

'Eight-thirty! Whew! I must have passed out completely last night.' Syrie's eyes went to the tray on the bedside chest. 'I'm being properly spoilt. The flowers are lovely. Thank you.'

During the night, the dusky-pink velvet curtains had been left drawn apart, and small, white-framed panes of glass were being lit up by the sun, which was casting rays right across the wide, upstairs veranda.

Ah . . . verandas, she thought—with a few old comfy chairs and tables. Maybe even a sofa and some potted plants. In so many parts of the world the veranda had survived its nineteenth-century British colonial beginnings of grand old pioneer houses and sugar estate mansions, such as this one.

As she ate a breakfast of fruit juice, fruit preserved in syrup and warm croissants and coffee, she gazed around the dramatic space which, although virtually drenched in pink roses and green leaves over black chintz, was not in the least overpowering, and wondered if the room had belonged to Blaine's mother.

When the phone rang beside her, she jumped and then waited a moment before lifting the receiver.

'Yes?'

'Good morning.' It was Blaine. 'So you're awake?'

'Yes, finally. I passed out last night, and now I'm being totally spoilt. I've been treated to breakfast in bed by Liselle.'

'Good.' His voice was abrupt. 'Let me put you into the rosy picture, Syrie. According to a telephone discussion this morning, your true love overlooked the date of your arrival, but will nevertheless, not be back today, nor tomorrow, as I had anticipated. He sends his apologies and hopes you will understand.'

'You should have put him through!' She lifted her voice in exasperation.

'What was the point, since he appears to have become so involved in Réunion? Besides, I didn't want you disturbed. You needed the rest.'

'Oh, Blaine!' She swung her legs off the side of the bed and stood up. 'How dare you do this to me? The fact that he's got the dates mixed and seems to have landed himself in some sort of backlog in Réunion doesn't give you the right to decide these things for me. Craig is going to be furious.'

'Don't be too sure of that, Syrie. Judging by the conversation we had, playing truant for the next couple of days will be well worth it but, knowing our friend Craig as I do, I'm sure he can justify anything. He'll have you eating out of his hand in no time. Look, when you're ready come down to the studio and meet the staff.'

A moment later, she slipped a pale cinnamon satin robe over the matching satin pyjamas she was wearing and, going out to the veranda, she gazed down at the garden, which was enveloped in a golden haze.

As Blaine had remarked, the house enjoyed spectacular views of the Indian Ocean and a curved white beach, which was framed by leaning palms. It was a place of untamed beauty, where washed-out skies seemed to play no part. Beyond the lagoon were savage coral rocks and underwater coral gardens and exotic fish.

Brooding on the fact that Craig was not expected for another two days, she turned and made her way back to the room, and then she took her time showering and dressing.

Liselle was putting the finishing touches to an arrangement of white daisies in the entrance hall, and Syrie was immediately reminded of the daisies in a basket at Craig's chalet, and this did not improve her mood.

'Liselle, where do I find the studio?' she asked.

'Come, I will show you. This way, *mademoiselle*. It is a beautiful day, no?'

'Absolutely super,' Syrie answered, trying to sound on top of the world.

The studio was a place of creative energy and talent, where white desks, slide projectors, stereo amplifiers, electronic flash units, tripods and even a computer were the order of the day. A white marble floor, inset with tiny rectangles of black, was highlighted by several oriental rugs, upon which the desks stood. French doors, with the usual small white-framed panes of glass, were open to the other section of Design Dimension. From where she was standing, Syrie could see two commercial artists at work.

Blaine seemed oblivious to her arrival on the scene, but somebody, who introduced himself as Andy Midrand, explained that they were busy mixing a sound track for an audio-visual presentation.

'You will be Syrie Knight, of course.' He held out a hand. 'We've all been expecting you. Welcome to Mauritius.'

'Thank you.' Syrie smiled pleasantly. 'I'm thrilled to be here.'

'Perhaps you would care to sit over here?'

Despite her now-screaming nerves, she kept smiling and then lowered herself into a white wicker chair and crossed her elegant legs. The green shirt she was wearing, with white jeans, echoed the colour of her moody eyes.

Blaine, she saw, was wearing white trousers with a white loose-knit shirt, and he looked like a doctor. His movements were restless and yet graceful and efficient. As he moved about the studio, his shoes made rubbery noises on the white floor. If he was aware of her, he still gave no indication of the fact.

There were more french doors open to the garden, which led from wide, curved steps. At one end of the studio a beige and chocolate beagle was curled up in a wicker basket, while a clumsy-looking labrador seemed perfectly aware of the fact that he was not permitted to enter the studio, and had flopped himself down on the steps.

Sensing Syrie's amused interest in the dogs, Andy said softly, 'The beagle is called Raizel and the labrador, for obvious reasons, is called Rascal. One wag of that tail and everything in this studio would go flying.'

Suddenly the music was switched off, and then, as if he had been aware of her presence all the time, Blaine turned and looked at Syrie.

Subjecting her to a brief, hard look, he came over to her while she unfolded herself from the white wicker chair.

'I see you and Andy have already introduced yourselves. Anyway, let me introduce you around,' he said, glancing at his watch.

To save face, she allowed him to do the necessary.

Craig phoned soon afterwards and asked to speak to Syrie.

'For you, Syrie,' Andy called out. 'From Réunion. Craig.'

With a glance at Blaine, she said, 'Excuse me.'

The moment she picked up the receiver Craig said, 'Syrie? Darling, is that really you?'

'Yes, believe it or not. I arrived *spot on time.*'

After a moment he said, 'You sound bitter, Sy.'

'Not bitter. Just unhappy.'

'I don't know how I forgot the date. You've got to believe this. In fact, for days on end I haven't even thought of the date. I've been under terrific pressure all round.'

'It's no good talking about it now, Craig. We'll talk when you get back in a couple of days' time.'

'That's what I'm ringing about, actually. We've managed to—catch up on everything. I've booked our seats and the plane touches down at two.'

'How nice. I'll see you then. Who will be meeting you, by the way?'

'My car is parked at Plaisance Airport. Don't worry about that. Bye, darling. Say you forgive me?'

'Of course. These things happen. Bye.' She replaced the receiver and then took a long breath. Her eyes went to Blaine.

'And so you intend forgiving him and abandoning yourself to those pent-up passions the moment he shows up? What changed his mind? I wonder. Guilt?' Blaine smiled sarcastically.

Her eyes were hostile. 'What's the point of this conversation? Apparently, Craig has managed to catch up and will be back on time, after all. Don't do this to me. I could do without the unsettling remarks which have been coming my way since we met at Plaisance Airport.'

He took her arm and said softly, 'Let's get out of here. Whether you like it or not, I want to talk to you.'

When they were in the hall, she said, 'We've got nothing to talk about, Blaine, except maybe small talk. Is this what you have in mind now? Small talk? Chit-chat?'

'Small talk has always irritated me. Let's go on the beach for ten minutes.'

Her immediate reaction was one of angry frustration. 'I don't want to go to the beach!'

'Oh, come, Syrie.' He glanced at his watch. 'I feel like a break. Besides, you'd like to see the beach, wouldn't you?'

'There's plenty time for that,' she replied quickly, but she began to walk with him. A few moments later, as she negotiated the wide steps which led down to the sand, she said, 'You are not without a certain treacherous charm.'

'Oh, why is that?' He turned to look at her.

'Back there, in the studio, it was—Syrie this and Syrie that. Little do they know what I have been going through as you've taunted me about Craig, who just seems to be the one to be messed around by Design Dimension. The more I hear, and see, the more sorry I feel for him.'

'You didn't sound sorry for him as you spoke to him on the phone.' He laughed shortly. 'Not bitter, Craig. Just unhappy.'

She stopped walking. 'I don't have to listen to this. What is more, I'm not going to . . .'

'Don't be so damned hasty. Craig is not for you. I'm telling you now. If you rush into this marriage, it will end on the rocks.'

'Let's talk about something else—or I'm going to turn back. So this is the beach?' She took a long breath and gazed around. 'It's very private, isn't it? You're lucky. It's almost like your own private Eden.'

Ignoring her remarks, Blaine went on, 'This started off quite the reverse, Syrie.'

'Oh, in what way? What are you getting at now?' She sounded as she felt—hostile.

'I had heard so much about Syrie Knight from Craig, that I was prepared to discover that I didn't like her.'

'*Really?*'

'Listen to me. When you phoned the studio, I was frankly irritated having to leave my work . . .'

She cut in quickly. 'You didn't have to leave your work. I told you at the time that I'd take a taxi. I'm not completely inexperienced when it comes to getting about on my own.'

'Well, the fact remains that I did come to the airport. If you're honest with yourself you will admit that something happened between us, *and* without any help from Greek bouzouki music.'

Realising how vulnerable she was, she said, 'What are you trying to say, Blaine? That the earth beneath our feet started to shake the moment our eyes met?'

'That is exactly what I am saying.' She caught her breath when he caught her by the shoulders. Before he kissed her he said, 'Why can't you be honest with yourself?' Drawing her closer, his hands travelled down the length of her back, so that her thighs were crushed against his.

Her lips responded almost immediately to the sensual exploration of his mouth, but when he released her she said, 'That was stupid, Blaine. Don't ever do it again, or you might get more than you bargained for.'

'Look, at least postpone the wedding for a month or two.'

'Can't you believe anything I say? I love Craig. Naturally, I have been frustrated and upset about what he has done—by forgetting the date—but I'm beginning to see how overworked he appears to be—how much under pressure. I'm trying to understand this. On the one hand you say that Craig spoke so much about me you were prepared not to like me on sight, and then, on the other hand, you show ignorance with regard to the date of my arrival. Surely *you* must have had *some* idea and checked this out with Craig before you sent him careering off to another island?'

As she spoke, however, she was aware of the warm sensations which were still surging through her body.

'You responded to me a moment ago. You know that,' he said, 'as well as I do.'

She lifted one shoulder. 'Maybe I did. So what? It's not the first time in my life that I've felt excitement at being kissed. It's just one of those things, let's face it!'

'I can't see you responding to every Tom, Dick and Harry who happens to come along.' He held her gaze, 'Shall we go?'

'Yes. Do you think Andy could drive me back to Craig's chalet?'

'Liselle is preparing lunch. You might as well stay here until your lover rolls up with his Girl Friday.'

'They've both just been on a shoot for Design Dimension, right? Don't try to unsettle me, Blaine. It won't work.'

Lunch was eaten in the dining-room in an aura of traditional refinement. Syrie's frustrated eyes went to the floppy crimson hibiscus flower which Liselle had placed on her side-plate.

Beyond the windows and french doors, there was an almost dream-like setting that included traditional white wicker veranda furniture and a garden which blazed with the colours of hibiscus, frangipani and bougainvillaea.

Conversation now revolved around Greece, sugar plantations in Mauritius, jet lag and Creole food. Blaine had adopted a cool attitude.

After lunch he went back to work and Syrie went to sit on a cane chair in the sun, and when a car arrived every muscle in her body seemed to go into a spasm.

It was Craig, of course, and the girl—dark-haired and dark-eyed, who had spent the night with him on the island of Réunion and, looking at them, as they got out of the car and came towards her, Syrie could believe just that. They both looked guilty, she thought.

Craig's handsome face went through a series of expressions. 'Oh, Syrie, what must you be thinking? You know, it's got so bad around here lately that—half the time—I don't even know the date. I completely forgot yesterday was the tenth.'

Mainly for Girl Friday's sake, she smiled. 'These things happen, let's face it.' She leaned back in the cane chair and put one tanned, slender arm over the side and swung her sunglasses, which she had taken off. All the time, she was aware of the other girl's eyes looking her over with cool and deliberate insolence, and this provoked her into saying, 'I suppose it was dim of me to assume you'd remember the exact date when you are so busy.'

Craig looked embarrassed. 'Sy, let me introduce you to Peta Faber.'

'Hi,' both girls said together, and then Peta said, 'Craigie, I'm going in. I'll get someone to come and help with our paraphernalia.'

'Our things must remain in the car, don't forget. Another thing, Pet, I want to leave as soon as possible.'

Peta gave him an angry glare. 'I know about our personal things. I'm talking about our photographic equipment. Don't forget—don't *you* forget, mister—that most of the curios we bought from that arts and crafts place belong to *me*.'

It was only after Peta—*Pet*—had gone that Craig put his arms around Syrie, who was standing now.

'How are you, darling? Huh? *Kalispera*, as we used to say in Athens.'

'I'm fine.' She made some pretence of clinging to him. 'As in Athens, *Efkharisto*. It seems a long time ago—Athens.'

Craig kissed her. 'Uhmm . . . I've missed you. We've got a lot to catch up on.'

After a few moments, they began to walk towards the wide steps which led to the veranda.

'What do you think of Blaine, by the way?' Craig sounded tense.

'What am I supposed to think of him—other than that he happens to be your partner? But it couldn't have been easy for him, having me on his hands. Once he took me to your chalet, I was quite prepared to stay there, but when he came back, he wouldn't take no for an answer, and here I am.'

They were in the hall now and she turned to Craig. 'I heard you say you intended leaving soon. My things are upstairs. While you're attending to matters in the studio, I'll go up and get them.'

'I'll come with you. I haven't said hello properly.' His grey eyes searched hers anxiously. 'I want to say how sorry I am. I couldn't do it—out there in the garden.'

Craig was tall, with sun-bleached fair hair, and he had

a gentleness about him which women, including Syrie, found attractive. Soon after meeting him, she had discovered that he was inclined to be moody and withdrawn, but this state of affairs, strangely enough, seemed to add to his charm. Once he'd said, 'I know I'm inclined to be moody. You'll have to be patient with me, Sy.'

'Why *are* you moody?' she'd asked lightly.

He'd thought for a moment and then laughed. 'I've never thought about it. I mean, a person doesn't go round asking oneself that kind of question, but now that I come to think about it—I have guilty childhood memories, I suppose.'

'Guilty about what?' She'd gone on smiling at him.

'Memories of never coming up to my parents' expectations, I suppose. Nothing I ever did was to their liking.'

'Oh, come, I don't believe that.' Her tone had been teasing and he had taken her into his arms and kissed her.

'That's because you're so in love with me you can't see through me, right?'

Now, in the room with the French four-poster and the rose-strewn chintzes and dusky-pink velvet curtains, he was taking her into his arms again. They kissed, tentatively at first, but becoming more urgent. When his hand went to her breast, she drew away.

'We'd better go downstairs,' she told him. Suddenly, she realised that Craig was not going to be content with anything less than her complete surrender *before* they were married, and the thought of going back to the chalet filled her with a kind of fright. Before she'd left Athens, she had come to terms that this was what actually would take place, for after all they were to be married soon after her arrival. It was only what she had expected, but now that the time was upon her she realised that she didn't want it to be this way—not right away. She needed time.

Craig stood back and lifted one mocking fair eyebrow. 'I'm the guy you've come to marry. Or have you forgotten?'

'I haven't forgotten,' she answered lightly. 'I still think we'd better go downstairs, though.'

'I hope you're not going to give me a hard time?' He smiled as he said it, but his eyes had narrowed.

Avoiding the issue, she said, 'Craig, will you carry this for me? I just want to check the bathroom. I'll join you in a minute.'

He waited in the hall for her. 'Leave your things here, Sy. Come through to the studio. Blaine must have introduced you around by now. Has he?'

'Yes, he has. Everybody seems very nice.' She wasn't as calm as she appeared.

Peta was scribbling on a clipboard, and she didn't look up as Craig and Syrie entered the studio. Syrie's eyes went to the other girl's jeans, which were stretched tightly across her hips and stomach, and the scarlet shirt which outlined her breasts, and then they came to rest on her pierced ears, which were adorned with dangling red crescent ear-rings. The diamond studs in Craig's bathroom belonged to a girl with pierced earlobes.

Completely ignoring Syrie, Blaine called out, 'Craig, did you remember to order that light-box before you left for Réunion? It hasn't arrived.'

'Yes, I did. I'll ring up before I leave and find out what's happened to it. It should have been here by now, but that's just typical.'

'Tell me when you're leaving,' Peta said rudely, 'since my car is at your place, I don't want to have to *walk* home.' She lifted her eyes and allowed them to slide over

Syrie, and there was no mistaking the hostility in their depths.

Well, bully for you, thought Syrie.

Still speaking to Blaine, Craig went on, 'I'll come in for a couple of hours tomorrow. After that, I'll be taking Syrie out to lunch somewhere.'

Syrie saw Blaine's handsome face freeze into a hard mask. 'In that case, leave those other transparencies with me,' he answered shortly. 'I'll go through them when I have a chance. Andy? Don't forget to caption that lot over there.'

'Captions can be like mini-ads in themselves.' Peta's voice was 'showing-off' and strident. 'More people read captions than body copy, actually.'

The drive to Craig's chalet had become strained the moment he'd opened the rear door for Peta.

'Oh, thank you, kind sir.' Her voice was stiff with childish sarcasm.

Later, Syrie felt her long, simmering look on the back of her neck, as she sat in front, next to Craig. Half turning, so that the question politely included Peta, she said, 'Was your trip to Réunion a success?'

It was Craig who answered. 'There were a few hassles to sort out, but it was successful. Photography is always tricky, but there were no calamities to speak of. We were given permission to photograph three models, in the volcano region.'

'Three models from Mauritius?' Syrie's mood lifted immediately. 'Did they go along with you, too?'

'They were Réunion models,' Peta said from behind. 'In other words, we met up with them there, took the necessary fashion shots at the volcano and said goodbye to them.'

'Who provided the clothes? Did you have to take them from *here*?' Syrie formed the questions casually.

'No,' Peta went on, 'the local branch of the main shop here supplied them.'

'It must have been very interesting.' Syrie glanced at Craig, but before he could say anything Peta answered.

'Let's face it, the trip was successful—and interesting enough for us to have been in a position of having time on our hands, and we felt so good about ourselves, we'd decided to go on a shopping spree and . . .'

'We finished earlier than expected.' Craig's voice carried a note of anger.

Syrie felt a sense of relief when they reached the chalet and then she tried not to show her resentment when Craig went out to the back garden to see Peta off.

When he came back to the patio, where Syrie had decided to wait for him, he said, 'One way and another, it's been quite a strain.'

'I'm sure it has. I mean, the volcano region must have been quite a strain alone.' Her voice was quiet.

'How do you mean?' He sounded puzzled. 'Are you making reference to the fact that it's *active*?'

'No. I mean—being "saddled" with three models must have been very trying to you.'

'What are you trying to say? That I wanted to be alone with Peta?'

'That's always a possibility, of course. Why are you getting so uptight, Craig?' She did her best to sound amused.

His temper soon flared up. 'Figure things out for yourself, Sy. I'm so damned pressed for time these days, I forgot the tenth.'

There was a trace of spite in her voice now. 'I'm embarrassed, really I am.'

He stared at her. 'Embarrassed? What about?'

'For putting you about.'

'Is that so? Well, it might just interest you to know

that I've done nothing but reproach myself since I found out what happened.' He held out his arms. 'But what are we going on about? Come here, darling.'

There was a pause, and then she said, 'No, Craig. *You* come *here*.' She smiled, though, when she said it, but her thoughts were on Peta's car which had been parked in the garden—for how long? Her mind was busy with diamond stud ear-rings, daisies in a basket and brass Indian bangles which might or might *not* have belonged to those articles which came under the list of 'Craig's collection'.

He was saying, 'Sy, what is this? How many times do I have to tell you I'm sorry? Shall I go down on my knees before you?' He laughed softly.

Syrie said sweetly, 'How long has she been staying here? It's something I've got to know.' She lifted her hands, 'I mean—I'm confused, dammit.'

'Just because her car was parked here? Come on, Sy. She often drives here from her place in the morning, parks her car here . . . I drive her to the studio and bring her back here after work, and she gets on her way.'

'It sounds—involved.' Her voice hinted at other matters which did not concern complicated transport methods.

'Oh, come. What is it you want? An in-depth report on my life, just because a girl happens to park her car in my garden?'

'In other words, you wish to disengage this conversation? Is that it?' She subjected him to another mocking smile, but she was angry inside. Angry and hurt. 'But, as you say—why go on like this? By the way, Blaine took my things through to your guest-room when I arrived. I think I'll go along and . . .'

'What's all this about the guest-room?' Craig's smile was disarming, but it left her cold.

'I'm quite comfortable in there. I'm sure you'll appreciate the fact that I'm feeling a little off centre at the moment. It's a . . .' She broke off and took a breath. 'Well, a case of getting to know you—all over again— in a way.'

'I'm glad you've said—in a way, Sy.' He sounded frankly hurt.

Later, he showed her round the chalet and she did not bother to enlighten him that she had seen most of it. Stopping in the kitchen to take a bottle of wine from the refrigerator, he said, 'We'll be going out to dinner later, of course, but is there anything you'd like? Smoked oysters—tinned—on biscuits?'

She fussed with the ends of her hair. 'I'm not hungry. *Efkharisto*.'

'Ah, that takes me back. I have a very weak spot for old Greece.' The relief in his voice was very noticeable.

'So have I—and the bouzouki music helped, of course.'

Craig missed the irony in her voice. 'Bouzouki music? I thought that guy played hits from the Beatles?'

She laughed suddenly, but it sounded brittle, even to her own ears. 'I wonder what made me think of bouzouki music?'

While they sipped wine, next to the splash pool, they began, slowly, to pick up where they had left off, and suddenly it seemed to be coming right. She told him about how utterly lost she'd felt after he'd left Athens, and he told her how hellish he'd felt in the plane, after take-off. She made him laugh when she described how she'd been hassled as she'd tried to get reasonable prices for some of the things she'd wanted to sell in Athens, and the ordeal of having other items packed and crated—ready for the island of Mauritius. 'You'll have a fit when you see what I've had sent over,' she told him. 'I hope you're in a good mood the day the crates arrive.'

'We'll open a shop,' he kidded.

'I hated selling my car,' she went on. 'I was really sad to see it go.'

'I have a reputation for enjoying buying and selling cars. I'll buy you another, my sweet.' He poured himself another glass of wine and then he turned to look at her. 'Talking about selling, I've sold the chalet, Sy. There was no time to write to you about it.'

She looked at him in amazement. 'What? But why?'

'I was offered a good price for it. It seemed too good to turn down.'

'When do you—we—have to vacate it?' she asked.

'Don't faint, darling—at the end of next week.'

Her green eyes were full of bafflement. 'Does—does Blaine know?' Why hadn't Blaine told her? she wondered.

'What has Blaine got to do with it?' Craig sounded stung.

She shrugged her shoulders. 'Well, nothing, of course. Why are you taking it this way, Craig?'

He came over to where she was sitting and, bending down, moved his lips over her forehead.

'You want to know something? I love you and I sat in that plane, coming back from Réunion, and I thought—how could I have been such a fool as to forget the date?'

His hair, she was quick to notice, smelled of cigarette smoke; although he did not smoke, Peta had been smoking in the back of the car.

'Well, I'm here. That's the main thing. But tell me, Craig, where will we go? Have you got another chalet in mind—lined up?'

He straightened up. 'Actually, before I went to Réunion, Blaine offered to put us up until after we're married. It will make no difference to him. It's a mansion of a place and he lives in it alone now that his old man has tied the knot again. Tell me, did you know it has a hundred and twelve doors?'

'I didn't go there to count doors.' She felt like fighting with him again.

'Let's just drop the sarcasm, Syrie, huh? We might end up having the reception there, as it so happens. I have made a provisional booking for the Poinsettia Room at the Bird of Paradise Hotel, which is very near here, but I think we'll skip that.'

'I think we *should* have the reception at this hotel, Craig.' She felt the need to escape his blustering and his drinking. 'I must go and unpack a few more things and then get ready for dinner.'

He came over to her and put his arms about her.

'I'm disappointed about the guest-room decision. You're a bundle of nerves, Sy. Why?' He kissed her, his mouth becoming insistent, as he sought her response. 'We're not going to wait, are we?' He drew back and looked into her eyes. 'After all, we're practically married, now that you're here. Why wait? In Athens—well, I could understand, to a point. You wanted to feel more secure with me—but now? In a matter of days you are going to be Madame Knox.'

'That sounds funny.' She laughed a little. 'I want to wait, though. You see, I don't want to feel—rushed. As you said, a moment ago, I am a bundle of nerves. I'll come right, don't worry.'

He was exasperated, though, by her unresponsiveness. 'Oh, come on, Sy. Forget about what happened, about my not being there to meet your plane.' He pulled her towards him and she felt his arousal and felt nothing but panic.

What had happened, she felt like saying, was that he had forgotten the date of her arrival; he had spent a night, on a neighbouring island where, according to Girl Friday, Peta, the shoot had been successful enough for them to have had time on their hands, even if that time had been cut short. Had they really finished early enough to have been able to board a plane today, or had Craig intended 'playing truant' for another few days? What was it Blaine had said? 'Knowing our friend Craig as I do, I'm sure he can justify anything. He'll have you eating out of his hand in no time.' Had *guilt* sent Craig flying back to Mauritius on the flight which had been intended from the beginning?

If the diamonds and the daisies and the car parked in the garden had anything to do with it, Craig had spent more than just one night with Peta.

'I can't help feeling tense, Craig. At least let me get settled in.'

'I thought you'd want me as much as I've been wanting you.'

'I do, Craig—but not now. I've just arrived. I'm not ready for anything to happen. I'm sorry, but there you are. If we rush things . . .'

'Whew, you're a cautious girl, Syrie. Tell me, are you mad about the sale of the chalet? Has this caused you to feel threatened in any way?'

'No. It's not really that. It's a whole lot of things.'

'We'll get a nicer chalet. One with two bathrooms.'

'One bathroom is fine. The bathroom in this chalet is very attractive. I love the daisies.' She felt a measure of satisfaction. 'And they've lasted beautifully, I see.'

He looked mystified. 'The daisies?'

'The daisies in a basket. Are they from the garden?' Her look was very innocent.

'Oh—those. Ah, yes. I have a man who comes once a week to tidy up a bit. I'm no gardener and don't profess to be. There's nothing much growing, though, except the usual island hibiscus, bougainvillaea, marigolds and a few tatty red, pink, yellow and white cannas—all shrivelled-up specimens.'

She knew he was drinking while she took a bath, and then she went through to the guest-room and looked out a bronze satin vest and a matching flared skirt, which were very simple and had been wildly expensive. When she was ready, she went to tell Craig that the bathroom was free.

'Maybe, now that I am ready, I'll have another glass of wine,' she told him, trying to sound cheerful.

'You trail the most exotic perfume, my love.' He smiled charmingly.

'Do I? It's strange how one never notices one's own perfume.' Her eyes went to the glass in his hand. 'Tell me, when do we begin to pack up here?'

'Pack?' He laughed shortly. 'By the looks of things, there won't be much left to pack. I've sold just about everything, and so, my darling one, you can go to town choosing exactly what you want for our new chalet. How's that? And then your own things will be arriving from Athens, and eventually from the UK. Your antiques. By the sounds of it, we'll be very comfortably off.'

'Craig, perhaps you'd better go and change. It's getting late and I'm beginning to feel famished.' Nothing, she thought, could be further from the truth.

'You're looking gorgeous.' His eyes went right over her and, putting his glass down, he came to put his arms around her. He laughed softly. 'Don't panic, Sy, I'm not going to crush your frock.' He nibbled her ear. 'Why won't you let me love you? We'll have something to eat here later. My canned food collection is equal to none.'

'Craig, we have our whole lives ahead of us. I've told you, I don't want to be rushed. I'm feeling—strange.'

'You know what?' he asked. 'I'll let you into a secret. I had you figured out in Athens . . . still, I'm prepared to wait. I promise. I'll be patient.'

'Good. Now go and change, please.'

The Bird of Paradise Hotel was set in a glorious tropical garden, and there were rough white walls, thatched roofs, palm groves and, explained Craig, during the day time, there were breathtaking views. He appeared to be quite sober now and she began to enjoy his company.

Before going through to the restaurant, which had a small dance-floor, they went to one of the cocktail lounges.

As Syrie hoisted herself gracefully on to a stool she said, 'I mentioned, in one of my letters, that I had to have a slight alteration done to my wedding dress. Remember?'

'Yes, you did,' he answered. 'What's it like, by the way?'

'Beautiful. It really is. I'm thrilled with it.'

'Am I going to be invited to a preview?' he asked, beginning to sound like the Craig she had met and fallen in love with in Greece.

'No, of course not. It's a secret. All I'm prepared to say, at this stage, is that it is absolutely stunning, as indeed it should be. I paid a lot of money for it.'

He reached for her hand and lifted it to his lips, kissing her fingers.

'Well, you have the money, and money is what it's all about. If you have the money—enjoy it.'

He was still kissing her fingers when Blaine Cartwright and an attractive girl arrived on the scene. It came quite naturally to Syrie to want to release her hand.

Craig stood up, 'Ah, Sister Hugo. You've taken time off to slip out of that tantalising little uniform of yours, I see? How are you, Hélène?'

'I am well, thank you.' Hélène's voice was low, with a French accent. 'And how are you, Craig?' Her eyes went to Syrie. 'Syrie, of course? We have heard so much about you.' Before either Craig or Blaine could perform the necessary introductions, she went on, 'I am Hélène Hugo. It's lovely to meet you.'

Vaguely, Syrie was aware of the fact that when Blaine had walked into the cocktail lounge he'd seemed to have taken ownership of it. Next to him, Craig's good looks seemed to have dwindled.

What followed was inevitable. After Syrie and Hélène had chatted for a few moments, Craig went along to the hotel restaurant to make arrangements for the bookings to be changed so that they could all dine at one table.

'Craig was saying recently, Syrie, that you might be having the reception here, at this hotel. Will you be expecting many relatives and friends to fly out here from England and Greece?'

'Believe it, or not, Hélène, I won't know a soul at my wedding, apart from you and the staff of Design Dimension which includes Blaine and my husband-to-be.' Syrie laughed lightly and reached for Craig's hand. 'It's a long way to expect people to come for a wedding. I'm not terribly sure about my aunt and uncle, though. They should be coming, but a lot depends on my uncle's health. My grandmother would adore to come, but she had a fall recently, which left her very shaken and unwell, although no bones were broken.'

'In this case,' Hélène answered seriously, 'I think a party is called for. What do you say, Craig? We can have it at Blaine's, for I am sure he will not mind. Would you, Blaine?' Hélène, dark-haired and with dark eyes, had a generous mouth and seemed to do a lot of smiling.

Blaine's expression became shuttered. 'Fine.'

Hélène went on, 'Craig can make out a list of friends he would like Syrie to meet before the wedding. That, to me makes sense.'

'That is because you are an efficient nurse,' Blaine replied. 'Would you like to dance?'

'I'd love to. Think about this, Craig and Syrie.' Hélène stood up and Syrie's green eyes followed them as they made their way to the dance-floor.

Blaine possessed an animal sensuality, she thought. The way he walked, so easily and loose-limbed. He had an air of physical strength, and yet his movements were graceful. As he took Hélène into his arms he said something to her, smiling down at her, for she was much shorter than he was.

The music stirred memories in Syrie's mind and, turning to Craig, she said, 'We danced to this in Athens. Do you remember? Everywhere we went, they seemed to be playing this tune.'

'Yes, I do. I do remember some things, believe it or not.' His eyes made impatient contact with hers.

'What is that in aid of?' she asked angrily.

'You keep reminding me what a useless so-and-so I am. In fact, you seem to delight in it.'

'But that's nonsense. You're being ridiculous, honestly. Let's stop this. I'd love to dance, actually.'

'Sure,' he shrugged one shoulder, 'if you think I'm capable.' He stood up, however, and held out a hand; after a confused moment she took it.

On the dance-floor, he kissed her. 'Forgive me, Sy? I'm sorry. I'm still smarting. I'll never forgive myself for forgetting to meet you at the airport.'

'Let's forget it. I have.'

'Really?' He gazed into her eyes.

'Really.'

Before ordering dessert, there was a *sega* demonstration, and then guests were invited to join in. At this point, Craig's moodiness was suddenly a thing of the past, and Syrie at last began to enjoy herself with him.

When the *sega* was over, they went back to their table and, soon afterwards, Craig asked Hélène to dance. Blaine gave Syrie a cool, assessing look.

She felt brittle. 'You don't have to ask me. I'd rather sit this one out, as they used to say.'

'Fine. That's suits me.' He sounded indifferent.

They were both quiet for a few moments, and then he surprised her by saying, 'Maybe you should live together first? For a while?'

'What is it with everybody these days, that they've got to live together first?' She gave him a hostile stare. 'I really don't go along with that. Living together can be bad news. Someone always ends up getting hurt.'

'The modern way, to pay court, seems to be sex before marriage, and in your case I'm inclined to agree. Maybe this way you'll get this guy out of your system. You don't owe him anything. You don't have to marry him, after all. It's no good rushing into marriage, just because you had a whirlwind affair in Athens.'

'Couldn't we talk about something else?' She picked up her glass and took a sip of her wine. 'One thing—I didn't come all this way to live with Craig. I came here to marry him.'

'If you marry him, you'll want out—eventually. Make up your mind for it.' He made an almost violent gesture.

'I can't understand you, Blaine. Craig is your partner.'

'Forget about that. You don't really love him but you've had to come here, though, to find this out. While you're making up your mind about him—live with him, if you must. By the way, has my partner told you he's sold the roof over your heads?' He drew the words out sarcastically.

Hotly, she answered, 'You seem to be enjoying this.'

He went on looking at her across the round table.

'*And* has he told you he's sold just about every stick of furniture?'

'He has told me everything there is to know.'

Blaine laughed shortly. 'I'll bet he has.'

She fought down a blaze of anger. 'He also told me that we have been offered a roof over our heads in a house which has a hundred and twelve doors but I have no intention of living in this house. I'm surprised you kept quiet about all this after you came to the airport for me. What I am trying to say is—I have no intention of staying in *your* house.'

'Famous last words, Syrie Knight.'

The music stopped and Craig and Hélène came back to the table.

'Well, have you and Blaine enjoyed your little chat?' Hélène asked, looking at Syrie.

'I was just telling Blaine that he should have been a script-writer for television soap operas. I think he's wasting his time with Design Dimension.'

'But, Blaine already writes scripts—not soap opera, of course. He writes scripts, daily.' Hélène sounded puzzled, and a little peeved.

'I'm just joking.' Syrie laughed lightly. 'Darling,' she looked at Craig, 'could we go now? I'm exhausted.'

'I think we'll stay on for a while. I'll be leaving for Réunion soon. I'll be doing midwifery at the hospital there, where I'll be working far too hard to play. We will stay, Blaine?'

'Of course, Hélène.' Blaine smiled back at her. 'The night is young.'

When they were in the car Craig said, 'Well, Sy, you and Blaine seemed to have a lot to say for yourselves—

and what's all this tripe about script-writing?'

'It was just a joke,' she answered.

'A joke against who? His partner? Craig Knox?'

'Craig, what is it with you? Why is everything suddenly going wrong?'

'So, you think everything's going wrong? Who's been changing your thoughts, Sy?'

They had reached the chalet. Syrie had refused to be drawn into a quarrel, and had remained silent while Craig had gone on and on airing his feelings.

He parked the car and turned to look at her.

'Why don't you say something? Are you going to sulk, Sy? Is this your way of making sure we don't land up in the sack together?'

She swung round. 'I'm not sulking. I'm just trying to make out what makes you tick, Craig.'

'Is that a fact? You seemed to know what made me tick in Athens, or have you forgotten? You're intent on making me feel a complete bastard. How is it you're so ready to think the worst of me? What am I? The certified dirty rat of Mauritius?'

'Craig, what you are—is your own worst enemy. Do you know that? What's got into you? Look, I've had enough. It's not my fault you've had a guilt-stricken childhood, all right? I mean, all this is so silly. Do you know what I'm going to do? I'm going to walk back and book into the hotel.'

'You'll do no such thing! Sy, I forbid you to get out of this car, unless it's to go inside with me. Look, I'm sorry, darling. I really am. Oh . . .'

She got out of the car and began to walk towards the chalet, and he followed her immediately. She stood to one side while he unlocked the door, and when they were inside he said, 'Darling, Sy, forgive me. I beseech you. You're driving me nuts, honestly. I've tried to explain—put it all down to the fact that I've been frantically busy. Blaine might have told you. Sometimes, when we have a deadline, we work half the night.'

'He did tell me.' Her temper was dying now. 'Maybe we'll both feel better in the morning, Craig. Less strung up. It hasn't been easy—you have to admit. We're both touchy. It's like meeting again—for the first time. It'll work out. Don't worry. Goodnight.'

To her relief, he made no attempt to stop her as she almost ran to her room.

CHAPTER FOUR

SYRIE slept fitfully. Lying awake for long spells, she listened to the sea noises when she was not brooding on the events which had led up to the present time in her life.

When Craig knocked on her door in the morning, she covered her eyes with the palm of one hand before she got up and reached for her satin robe.

For a moment she felt despair, and then she called, 'Coming. Just a minute.'

At the door he said, 'Good morning. I've brought you some coffee.' His cool grey eyes were accusing. 'Your door was locked. Why, Sy?'

She went back to sit on the edge of the bed. 'I don't want to talk about it.'

'So, you don't want to talk about it? Well, I *do* want to talk about it, since what you did was nothing but an affront. I can't understand your phoney scruples. If you're so paranoid about us sleeping together before we're married, which will be soon enough, let's go off to Port Louis today, and get the marriage vows over and done with.'

Woman-like, she immediately thought about her stunning wedding dress and the wide-brimmed, lacy hat which she'd looked after so carefully on the flight from Paris.

'That's not what I want. It's not what you want, either, if you're honest, Craig. Have you forgotten how we talked about this in Athens? How we planned? As a

68

result, I went to considerable expense and bought a wedding dress and a lovely hat, since I didn't want a veil.'

He surveyed her with some impatience.

'Well, that's no problem. We could have the reception at a later date.' He lifted his arms. 'I mean, what *is* the problem here?'

'Another thing, Craig . . . I wouldn't talk about phoney scruples if I were you. What's phoney about coming here to marry you?' Her green eyes were hostile. 'Since arriving in Mauritius, I have been subjected to a lot of tension. My trust in you was shaken. A lot of women would have just grabbed their bags and boarded the very next plane back to Athens.'

He sighed loudly and lifted his shoulders.

'OK, from now onwards it will be one day at a time. One night at a time. One minute at a time, if that's what you want. Come through when you're ready. There's a little patio off the kitchen. We'll have breakfast there.'

As she sipped her coffee, she tried to sort out her conflicting thoughts. When she went through to the bathroom, she noticed that the diamond studs were gone. So were the daisies and the L'Oréal mousse.

Craig was busy in the kitchen, which was filled with the aroma of fresh coffee and warmed croissants.

'Mmm . . . smells good.' She did her best to inject a little joy into the situation. 'Has your cleaning lady arrived? What's her name again? Armetta?'

'That's right. Armetta. No, she arrives later.' Craig's expression was remote. 'Are you ready for some breakfast?'

The smile on Syrie's face felt stiff. Obviously, she was thinking, *he* had removed the objects from the bathroom.

Still in that same artificial voice, she said, 'I'm famished. Though I'd better start watching my weight, if I want to get into that wedding dress.'

They went out to the patio. It was a sparkling day and she had decided to wear a button-through purple denim skirt and shirt, which she had teamed with a silk emerald-green scarf. The shirt was wide and square and could be warn as a jacket, which was how she had decided to wear it, over a matching bra and with only two buttons done up and the rest hanging loose. When she moved, or when the breeze caught at the shirt, there were tantalising glimpses of her tanned midriff and the emerald-green silk sash on the waist-band of the skirt. Four heavy gold bracelets jangled on her wrists. Her tanned legs were bare and she wore strappy purple sandals.

'I've been thinking, Sy . . . Let me go ahead and arrange for a civil marriage ceremony to take place as soon as possible. How does that suit you? Being married in church will, as you know, mean that the banns must be read on three Sundays. Personally, I can't see the point of going through all that. Everything else will remain the same, though. In other words, we'll still have the reception at a date which will fit in with our Club Med booking at Réunion. I'll take Blaine up on the offers he made before you arrived. That means we'll have the reception at his house. It might be a good idea to hire a marquee, not to mention a jazz quartet and caterers, of course. Liselle and Armetta can make themselves useful for a change.' Craig sat back in his chair and gave Syrie a long, assessing look.

She appeared cool and poised but, beneath that polished exterior, there lay nothing but sheer disappointment, mingled with a kind of rage that Craig should be doing this to her.

After a moment she said, 'Why does everything we do have to involve Blaine Cartwright? I'm afraid I—I—don't like him. Why can't we have the reception at the Poinsettia Room? After all, you mentioned the Poinsettia in the first place. I should have thought that would solve everything—the hassle of a marquee, the caterers—*Blaine* . . .'

'Blaine offered, Syrie. I explained that. He offered before you arrived.'

'Yes, that might be, but now that I *have* arrived, I don't see why we should have to rely on him. Let's have the reception at the hotel and, by the way, I'd prefer to stay at the hotel after we leave this chalet. What's so urgent about going to stay in his house, until we leave for our honeymoon? It just doesn't make sense.'

'I'm afraid it makes a lot of sense, Sy.' Craig's voice was only *slightly* mocking.

'Why is this?' Her voice was cool.

'Well, I'll be perfectly honest with you. I have a problem. You see, I'm trying to cut down on expense. Design Dimension has eaten up a lot of my capital. I'm sorry, but there it is. It's been a big drain on my finances, actually.' He raked his fingers through his fair hair.

Syrie lifted her glass of pineapple juice. 'Oh, I see.' Her voice was soft. 'I—ah—didn't realise, of course. I'm sorry. Won't you let me help in some way? I mean, that's only fair. I don't expect you to pay for everything. In fact, I never have. I always intended to play my part.'

There was a pause, and then he said, 'Thank you. That's jolly decent of you. We'll talk about it, OK? Maybe . . .'

'Craig, is Design Dimension in some sort of trouble?'

'No. No, no. Actually, it's flourishing. It's just that it has eaten into my capital, good and solid. It's been like feeding the one-arm bandit machines in a casino, in a way.' He laughed a little, but went on, 'You know what it is. I bought my way into the business, and the more I put in, the more seems to be expected of me.'

With barely concealed anger she said, 'I admire you for going into Blaine's business, but when is he going to let up? You must be like a godsend to him, honestly.' Her anger against Blaine grew. Blaine seemed to accept the fact that Craig was overworked and contributing so much. After a moment she said, 'Could I make a condition?'

'Sure. Go ahead.' Craig sounded wary.

'After we get back from our honeymoon and settled in another chalet, I'd like us to receive the blessing of the church. In fact, I want that—very much.'

Suddenly, he laughed. 'That's sneaky.'

'Sneaky? In what way is it sneaky?'

'Well, you'll be putting me through getting married twice.'

'Oh, I see. Aren't I worth it?' She smiled, when she asked this.

'Of course.' He stood up and came over to her. 'You should know that by now. Haven't I been doing my best to make it up to you?' He kissed her.

Soon after breakfast they left, and the scenic drive to Blaine's old plantation house was short. Syrie gazed at the foaming white line, just offshore, and experienced the magic of the island. The range of green, in the way of palms, trees and grass alone, amazed her—lime, emerald and neutral tones. Cannas, in Gauguin colours, grew wild on the roadside. She forced herself to unwind.

As he parked the car Craig said, 'You'll have to come into the studio, I'm afraid. I may be some time.'

'Perhaps I'd better wait in the garden?' she told him.

'Look, Sȳ, let's be happy. OK?'

'If anyone wants to be happy, Craig, I do.'

'Well, why aren't you? Come on.'

Blaine, she saw, was wearing huge glasses which, as it so happened, only seemed to add to his good looks—and as Craig and Syrie entered the studio he completely ignored them.

'Peta,' his voice was loud and irritable, 'how about fitting those slides into a circular tray? They should have been attended to an hour ago.'

Peta looked at Blaine in astonishment. 'What? All of them?'

Blaine swung round. 'Well, of course—all of them. I've been trying to get that into your head. What do you think they're there for?'

As Peta brushed past Craig she hissed, 'Blaine's being absolutely impossible. You don't have to be mad to work in this place, but it sure helps. Sometimes, I ask myself why I stick it—why I allowed you to talk me into coming and working here in the first place.'

Syrie began to feel in the way. 'I'll wait in the garden, after all, Craig. Things look, and sound, a bit hectic in here.'

'Fine. I'll be with you as soon as I can.' As Peta moved away he said softly, 'And try to be happy. *Think* about being happy, darling.'

She gave him a level look. 'I spend a lot of time thinking about being happy.'

'Well, maybe you should just try to be and get on with it.'

The garden was beautiful and Syrie's mood began to improve, until she saw Blaine coming towards her about fifteen minutes later. The electric-blue eyes, as she had come to think of them, held hers. They were also angry and flecked with gold.

He went straight to the point. 'So, you've decided on a civil marriage, no less?'

She was immediately on the defensive. 'Yes, we've changed our plans.'

'In other words,' his voice was hard and mocking,

'you've decided not to waste time. There will be no reading of the banns on three Sundays to give opportunity of objection.'

'And—who would object? You?' She gave him a withering look before she turned her back on him.

'You never know what I might do,' she heard him say before he reached for her and pulled her round to face him. 'Tell me something, Syrie. What exactly were your feelings when we met at Plaisance Airport?'

Thinking of how hard Craig appeared to work, her green eyes were blazing.

'Do you mind? Let go of me, Blaine.'

'No. Not before you tell me. Now, be honest. What is more important, be honest with yourself.'

Looking back at him, she wondered whether she should be honest and tell him that she had felt excited in a way she had never been before—which was ridiculous!

'Oh, stop being so dramatic, Blaine. I can't stand any more.'

His grip on her arms tightened and the touch of his warm fingers tantalised her senses.

'Tell me, Syrie.'

'I don't remember, and that's a fact.'

'You honestly don't remember?' His lips appeared hard and ruthless, but she was fully aware that they were really very sensually chiselled.

'No.'

'Well, then, allow me to refresh you memory.' He drew her close and wrapped his arms about her, his thighs touching hers.

She was at this moment honest enough—*with herself*—to accept that what she was feeling was an overwhelming desire to be possessed by Blaine Cartwright—one dark and stormy night.

Against her mouth he said, 'Come on, what did you

feel?' The arrogance of his next kiss was calculated. 'What are you feeling now? Huh?'

She fought against him—before her body became drained of all reasoning power. Blaine released her abruptly. 'Go on, tell me.' His eyes pierced hers. 'Just for the record.'

'Just for the record, I *suppose* I felt excited about you. That's all. After all, you're arrogant—that stands out a mile—you're handsome and devilish and—ah—sexual; always a dangerous and romantic combination where women are concerned—in a way women find threatening. I felt threatened and it's nothing I'm ashamed of, actually—but that's all there was to it.'

'Therefore . . . forget about this guy,' he said callously.

'Nothing has changed. I love *this guy*, as you will persist in referring to him. He's probably wondering where I am, right now.' She turned to go.

To her surprise, he did not follow her, and when she got back to the studio Craig was talking to Peta. As Peta turned her petulant young face to one side, there was the twinkle of a small diamond stud ear-ring. Earlier on, her ear-rings had been red. Obviously, thought Syrie, Craig had returned her diamonds and she had lost no time in putting them back on. She felt hot rage at the look of pure insolence which Peta was directing at her.

One of the phones started ringing and Andy Midrand called out, 'Peta? Why can't you answer that? I can't take another call. I think I mentioned that . . . '

'Oh, for Pete's sake, let's get out of this lot.' Craig touched Syrie's arm.

In the car she said, 'The least you could have done was to get rid of her things.'

He turned to look at her. 'What are you talking about now?'

'You know very well what I'm talking about—I'm

talking about the diamond ear-rings. I'm talking about the daisies and the L'Oréal mousse, not to mention that cute little red car which was parked in your garden.' She kept quiet about the brass Indian bangles, since they had been in his bedroom and she did not want to be accused of snooping.

He laughed lightly. 'So that's what's bugging you? Oh, come, Sy. Now, what am I supposed to say about these things?'

'I want to hear about this girl. Peta!' she lashed out at him. 'Peta Faber! Girl Friday!'

'She is—and you've hit the nail right on the head—just that. Girl Friday and it's all very innocent, believe it or not.' After a moment he went on, 'Look, Peta did spend the night in question in the chalet, but there it ended. There was nothing in it. She stayed there for the simple reason that we were leaving early, on this shoot, the next morning. We were using my car to go to the airport. I left it there, as you know. Is it your aim to go on making me feel like a first-class bastard, Syrie? I can't seem to do anything without you criticising me. Why can't you trust me?'

Very softly she said, 'I *want* to trust you.'

'Well, as I keep saying, why don't you give it a damn good try? In any case, let me put you into the picture. Peta's got a boyfriend. In fact, they spent a weekend at my place while I was away recently.'

Syrie gazed out of the window at the changing colours of the sea. 'Have you forgotten that I trusted you enough to come to Mauritius to marry you?'

'No, I haven't forgotten. What's got in the way, though? A girl I happen to work with? A girl who drifts frustratedly into one relationship after another? What do you take me for?' His laugh was mocking. 'Come on, darling. Don't sulk. I love you. I've told you that. Look, I have the addresses of two chalets. I told you about it. We'll look over one of them before we have lunch somewhere. After lunch, we'll drive around so that I can show you a bit of Mauritius, and then we'll view the second chalet.'

As it turned out, the chalet would not have suited them, for each bedroom was the size of a dormitory at a hostel. It was obviously a chalet meant for a large family, or a group of friends. It was attractive enough, however, to improve Syrie's mood and to inspire them both to go on searching until they found a chalet to suit them.

They had lunch and then drove to a blissful stretch of coastline, and the beauty of it led Syrie to decide that Mauritius was where she wanted to settle with Craig.

It did not take long to realise that the second chalet, which was ideally close to the studio in Blaine's house, was just what they wanted, and they agreed there and then to rent it directly it became vacant. Unfortunately, that would be some time after their honeymoon was over.

That night, they dined at the Bird of Paradise Hotel, and soon after they got back to Craig's chalet he wanted to make love to her. Languid with having had too much wine to drink, she allowed him to lift her up and carry her through to his bedroom.

'Why are you so nervous?' Craig nibbled her ear. 'We're as married as dammit, Sy.'

'I know,' she whispered, as he moved his hand from her arm, which he had been stroking, to her thigh. They were both quiet for a moment, looking at each other. He began stroking her thigh and closing her eyes, she turned and clung to him.

'I want to undress you; look at you . . . I want you, so much . . . let me . . .' He groaned. 'Oh, Sy—let me, darling . . .'

As he began to undress her he went on kissing her, while one part of her wondered whether he had done this to Peta Faber, in this same bed. Somehow, she felt he had and she began to lose her hold on her excitement, but it took him a few moments to realise that she had lost interest in making love.

Drawing back angrily, he said, 'What is it?'

After a moment, she said dismally, 'I can't. I thought I wanted to, but . . .'

'Don't stop me now, Sy. You can't! Have mercy, woman.' He began stroking her again, trying to get her to respond, but she grabbed his hand and held it.'

'Don't, Craig. I don't want to. I'm sorry.' She took a long, unsettled breath. 'Something just got in the way.'

He rolled away from her. After a moment he said, 'By something, you mean Peta. Right?' There was real anger in his voice now. 'I'll be honest with you now. Even though you hung out in Athens, you still struck me as being pretty liberated.'

Her own temper flared up. 'In what way—*liberated*?' She sat up and reached for the jacket which she had been wearing, and shrugged her arms into the wide sleeves.

'Well, you'd knocked about.'

'What do you mean? I'd knocked about? Perhaps you'd care to explain?' Her voice was like thin ice, ready to crack.

'Well—from one country to another—working here, working there. Then, from what I gathered, you moved on—new faces, new jobs. You know something? You've always—from the word go—struck me as being too independent to care about anyone except yourself, and tonight has proved it.'

'Really? Go on, Craig. Let's get everything out in the open. You tell me what you did before you met me, and I'll tell you. Tell me what you've been doing since

I first met you. I'll tell you. Another thing, don't you think . . .'

He cut in. 'Another thing, don't *you* think it was a bloody stupid way to set about squandering an inheritance?' His grey eyes went over her face.

She was staggered. 'I just don't get any of this. Is this some kind of bad dream? What has my inheritance got to do with anything?'

He was beside her in a flash. 'I'm sorry I said that, Sy. It was totally uncalled for. Forgive me, but are you ever going to believe anything I say?'

'I don't want to talk about it—this awful subject.' She wondered if Craig was using her in some awful way that had nothing to do with love. Her suspicions would not go.

'I don't know why in hell I said that, Syrie. Look, I'm not that devious, believe me. At this moment, though, I'm feeling rejected—or can't you understand that? I wanted to hurt you.' He battled to turn her round to face him, but she held herself stiffly and would not turn her face to him.

'Syrie,' he was almost shouting now, 'what can I do to make you understand? I love you. Do you hear?'

She was silent for several moments, and avoided looking at him. Finally she said, 'We're both on edge. I can see that, but I'd like to go to my room now. There's a lot we have to work on—like getting to know one another all over again. It's going to be hard . . .'

'You keep saying that, but—I suppose you're right. Just go, Sy. I—er—I've had it, right at this moment.'

She lay awake, hour after hour. In the morning, however, Craig's gentle magnetism got to work on her again, and they even began to enjoy the kind of relationship they had experienced in Athens.

The cocktail party in her honour—where she was

to meet a number of Craig's friends, before the wedding,
was to take place the following day. On the spur of the
moment, while Craig was at the studio, she decided to
phone Blaine.

'It's Syrie,' she said, a little breathlessly. 'Hi.'

'Does this have to be right now?' At the sound of his
voice, she felt her stomach muscles tighten. 'I have a lot
on my mind.'

'Well, I won't keep you.' Her voice was stiff. 'Hélène
phoned yesterday. Apparently she is going to visit her
family, because of illness, and although she says everything has been taken care of, so far as the party is
concerned, I wondered what I could do to help Liselle.
Should I come over?'

'Liselle is quite capable of seeing to everything,'
Blaine answered curtly.

'I know Liselle is capable, Blaine, but it does seem a
little unfair to . . . '

He cut in on her. 'Look, I'm busy right now, Syrie.
You don't have to bother about anything. Hélène is very
efficient and has seen to everything. Have a nice day.'

When he rang off, Syrie took the receiver from her ear
and gazed at it in disbelief.

Shocked at the insult, she kept this news from Craig,
but she did say, that evening, 'I wish there was
something I could do to help with the party, especially
as Hélène has been called away.'

'Why should you help?' Craig answered. 'The party is
for you. Besides, there's Liselle. What's Blaine paying
her for? For that matter, Armetta can be roped in.'

She did not tell him what had taken place the *day
before*, when the Creole lady had said, 'I work no more.
From tomorrow—no more, until *monsieur* pays me.' Her
voice was blunt and to the point.

Syrie had felt her eyes widen. 'Has he not paid you,

Armetta?'

'But I have just informed. He has not paid me.' Armetta held up three fingers. 'For three months. I am now in a black mood. I have a sick husband.'

'Three months! He must have totally forgotten.' Syrie ran her fingers through her hair. 'I will let you have your money, Armetta. Just tell me how much it is.'

Armetta looked stricken. 'This money you will recover from *monsieur*?'

'Of course, Armetta. I'm just terribly sorry this has happened. He'd be so ashamed if he suddenly realised what he's done. Please don't mention it to him. He is so busy lately. He's under a lot of pressure.' Syrie forced herself to laugh lightly. 'When I am his wife, I will boss him around and I will see to it that, no matter how busy he is at the studio, it will not happen again. He's very naughty.'

On the evening of the cocktail party, Syrie decided to wear a dress which hung from her shoulders and arranged itself in champagne-tinted silken folds. A heavy gold belt hung loosely on her hips. Her tawny hair was turned inwards and hung forward, brushing her jaw line. When Craig saw her he said, 'Darling, you look wonderful, but then, you always do.'

'Thank you.' She smiled back at him and made up her mind to relax.

They were on the veranda of Blaine's house, on their way into the hall, when Peta called out from the far end.

'Craigie, could I have a word with you, in private?'

Beside her, Syrie felt Craig stiffen.

'Does it have to be now? We've arrived late as it is.'

'I won't keep you.' Peta sounded aggressive.

Craig took an impatient breath. 'Sy, I won't be a minute, OK? Unless somebody grabs you, wait for me in the hall. I'd better see what she wants, before there's a scene.' He laughed softly, but he sounded on edge.

Syrie was stunned by such calculated rudeness on Peta's part. She must have been waiting here for Craig to arrive, she thought furiously.

In the hall she met Andy Midrand. 'Hello, Syrie. You're looking very sleek and lovely.' He glanced towards the open double doors. 'Where's Craig?'

'He stopped to talk to Peta. They're on the veranda.' She hoped he would not see the angry frustration which she knew must be obvious in her eyes.

'Oh, I see.' Surprise was in Andy's voice, however. 'In that case, perhaps you should come through and I'll begin to introduce you around, until Craig is there to take over.'

When Craig finally arrived on the scene he said, 'I'm sorry, Sy, but when Peta makes up her mind about something, there's no stopping her.'

'Was it something about work?'

'Well—ah—yes, actually. I hadn't forgotten you, though. I looked in, but saw that Andy had taken you under his wing. Did you meet Hilly—his wife?'

'Yes, I did.'

'And . . . ' Craig glanced around the elegant room. 'What about Belinda and André Ricosta—the couple next to that huge floral arrangement?'

'We've been introduced, Craig.' She did not tell him that she had already had a long chat with Belinda Ricosta and had ended up confiding in the tall, glamorous girl. She'd found herself explaining how tense she was and how she seemed to be doing nothing but bicker with Craig—how nervous she was.

Belinda had laughed. 'Nerves, my dear Syrie. Nerves. Forget about being liberated—when it comes to getting married, we women go to pieces. I was totally out of love with André. I was jealous, suspicious—like a young schoolgirl going through her first crush. I can't tell you. It was so *unlike* me.'

Peta came into the room and Syrie found it intolerable that this girl should look at her with such cool insolence plastered all over her face. Turning to Craig, she said, 'I'm trying very hard, Craig, to understand what is going on. Or should I say—*Craigie?* What is it with this girl? Why didn't you have the courage to tell her that you would talk to her later?'

'She gets hysterical, that's why. She's having boyfriend trouble. Actually, she asked me whether they could use the chalet while we are on our honeymoon. I had to explain I'd sold it. She's all mixed up.' He glanced around. 'I'm surprised at Blaine. He might have "shown face". I know he was supposed to be driving Hélène to her folks, but surely he must be back by now?'

'Don't worry about it,' Syrie answered. 'Rudeness seems to be a Blaine Cartwright trait, or haven't you noticed? I'm just sorry the party had to be in his house in the first place.'

When Blaine finally arrived, he unnerved her by giving her a long look before he came over to where she was standing with Craig.

'We were wondering where you'd got to.' Craig's voice was accusing and he moved away to talk to the Ricostas.

Syrie found herself alone with Blaine and he reached for her glass. 'This looks past its prime, and what is more you don't seem to be enjoying it. Let me change it for something else.'

'I'm not enjoying it, as a matter of fact. It's something Craig had the bartender fix for me.'

'I think a change of bartender is indicated. Besides, I want to talk to you. Let's go along to the study.'

'I don't see what we have to *talk* about, Blaine, unless
it's the weather? As it so happens, I have something to
say to *you*, though.'

'Well?' He lifted his shoulders and gave her a mocking
smile. He found a place for her glass and then took her
arm.

Directly they reached the study, he closed the door
and she watched him as he went behind the bar counter
and poured a drink for her and one for himself.

As he came round and passed the glass to her, he said,
far too casually, 'Tell me, why did *you* have to pay for
the honeymoon air-fares to Réunion?'

Syrie stiffened. 'Who told you I paid for them?'

'Let's just say I found out, just as I also happened to
find out that Craig has got you to open a store account,
in your name . . . in Curepipe.'

She was furious that she had been put on the
defensive. 'It's got nothing to do with you, but since you
have the audacity to ask, Craig had not yet collected his
new card from the bank. I will be using the store account
when it comes to choosing items for our new home,
since most of the time Craig will be working.'

'I see.' He rubbed his chin with the palm of one hand.
'Well, don't be surprised if he uses it on the sly.'

She matched his sarcasm. 'Is that all you had to say?'

'For the moment.' He lifted his glass to his lips.

'Well, I have something to say to you, Blaine. I have
also been putting two and two together but, unlike you,
I feel I have *reason* to interfere. It has become quite clear
to me that Craig never seems to stop putting money into
Design Dimension. It is obvious that you are taking
advantage of his easy nature; and that goes for shoving
unnecessary work on to him as well. It's time you started
thinking about these things, instead of trying to work
out how you can smash his relationship with me. That's

the only reason I have come along to the study.' She put her glass down on the counter and made for the door, but before she could open it he was there.

'Blaine, do you mind? I want to get out of this room as quickly as possible—before I say something I'll regret.'

Taking her by the shoulders, he turned her around, so that she had her back to the door, and then he placed both hands against the door, trapping her. She looked at him furiously.

'What defeats me is, although Craig happens to be your partner, you don't seem to trust him.'

'Until recently, Syrie,' Blaine's voice sounded heavy, 'I've always trusted him. It was just by chance, a couple of weeks ago, that my suspicions were aroused and I became wise to the fact that Craig has been helping himself, very cunningly, to the firm's money. To what extent, I'm not yet sure, and our accountants have begun to work on this. I'm prepared to bet, though, that it will be quite a sum.'

After a shocked moment she said, 'I don't believe any of this. Why are you telling me these awful things? Why don't you go straight to Craig—but maybe I should answer that question for you? Since Craig has been investing more than his fair share of money, maybe you should look elsewhere for the culprit. I trust Craig—even if his partner doesn't.'

'Maybe the time is ripe for you to begin to ask yourself if you *should* trust him. Take time off to think about this. After all, there's no need to rush into marriage, just because you slept with the guy in Athens.'

'I don't have to listen to this. When did you make this discovery—that Craig was helping himself to funds? On the day our eyes were supposed to have met and clung together at Plaisance Airport? You were totally unconcerned that Craig was overworked, then, just as he is now, and that he is forever pumping money into Design Dimension.'

Blaine's laugh was harsh. 'Did he tell you this?'

'You can't bear to see Craig happy, can you, Blaine? Or me!' Without stopping to think, she slapped his handsome hard face and she was immediately appalled at what she had done. She stared at him with shocked green eyes.

'Don't you ever try that again, Miss Syrie Knight. I'm warning you—I'm very likely to reciprocate.'

'Have you quite finished?' she asked. 'Because if you have I would like to open the door.'

Behind her back, someone was trying to open the door and, swearing softly, Blaine dropped his arms.

'Sorry,' Andy Midrand was saying cheerfully. 'I was just looking for Hilly. She has a headache and has gone off somewhere.'

Craig was looking for her when she got back to the drawing-room. Looking at him, Syrie thought that his grey eyes always seemed to hold all the innocence of a young boy, and she felt suddenly very sorry for him. She found herself accepting that he was having far too many demands made on him by Blaine Cartwright. No wonder Craig was forgetful and vulnerable, to the point where he was suspected of having swindled his partner.

'You look so tired, Craig.' She stroked his cheek, while anger towards Blaine boiled within her.

He laughed a little. 'Well, let's face it. I *am* tired.' He reached for her hand and kissed it. 'Going into partnership with Blaine has been anything but easy. As I've explained, it's been a case of money, money, money; but let's talk about something else, darling.'

They stood talking quietly, hemmed in by guests who were standing about in clusters, holding drinks and snacks and having a lot to say for themselves.

CHAPTER FIVE

TWO days later, and much to Syrie's reluctance and concern, they moved into Blaine's shuttered plantation house. Except in the event of a severe tropical storm, the shutters were mostly always open.

The household items, which Craig had decided to keep, were now stored in the outbuildings of a small shop belonging to a Creole couple nearby. Armetta had gone on leave and would return to help them to move into their chalet and to continue working as housekeeper, as Syrie fully intended to find work.

Since they were not yet married, Liselle showed them to separate rooms. Syrie was back in the dramatic pink and black room with the magnificent French four-poster, and Craig had been given a room and bathroom at the end of the corridor.

Blaine, who must have been in the studio, did not put in an appearance, but Andy Midrand, cheerful as ever, was there to say hello.

'So you've sold the chalet, Craig? I was surprised to hear that. Was it something you decided on in a weak moment?'

'No, it wasn't. As a matter of fact, I had sold it before Syrie arrived. I was hoping to be in a position to move into another chalet before she arrived, but I'm afraid it didn't work out that way. However, we have found just the place we want. Syrie's thrilled with it.' Craig turned to look at her. 'Aren't you, darling?'

'I love it,' she answered. 'There's going to be a lot to do when we get back from our honeymoon, but it will be fun.'

Apart from meal times, she hardly saw Blaine during the following hectic days. She seemed to be whirling from one place to another. The caterers had been difficult to work with. Gifts kept arriving and Hélène Hugo sent an apologetic letter from her mother's home to say that she was leaving for Réunion earlier than she had anticipated and, much to her disappointment, would not be coming to the wedding. A gift from Hélène arrived the next day.

Syrie found herself running through check-lists. Cars and small vans began to arrive, delivering items which had been ordered for the reception. The cake, a multi-tiered delight, arrived. The florist arrived with buckets filled with flowers, which were to be transformed into beautiful arrangements.

A very blue-eyed, angry-looking Blaine was full of restless energy whenever she saw him, and so she tried to avoid him.

At the end of it all, she woke up one morning and thought—well, this is it. This is my wedding day.

Sea noises drifted through open windows and french doors, and she lay back on her pillows, listening.

Then she took her time bathing and dressing very slowly. When she was ready, she would go downstairs to the huge hall with its black and white floor in a geometric design, and its stairway of vast proportions. The chandelier with its sparkling prisms would have been turned on and glittering overhead. They'd planned it all. Craig would be waiting for her, along with the judge who was coming to Blaine's house to marry them. Andy Midrand and his wife were going to act as witnesses. The short ceremony had been scheduled to take place at noon, and the reception was to follow soon after. The plane to the island of Réunion was scheduled for six o'clock.

She kept going out to the long veranda where she could look down upon the scene of the reception. A red carpet led directly from the foot of the downstairs veranda steps to the huge marquee which had been erected on the lawn. Some of the guests, she knew, would stand on either side of the carpet, waiting to congratulate the newly married couple after photographs had been taken on the gracious steps. Later, women would most certainly rave over her wedding dress and her lacy, wide-brimmed hat.

Andy was to read the telegrams, and many of them would have arrived from relatives and friends who could not be there to see her married on the island of Mauritius.

As she thought about these things, Syrie brooded on the fact that her wedding day had been marred in many ways. For one thing, she and Craig had argued bitterly about moving to Blaine's house.

'It will only be a matter of days,' Craig had said, 'and then we'll be out of his house and on our honeymoon. When we get back we can move into some hotel nearby. I'll make the necessary reservations from Réunion.'

'I can't see the point of all this,' she'd argued. 'Everything seems to revolve around Blaine Cartwright. *Why?*'

'Because Blaine just happens to be my partner, that's why. For heaven's sake, Sy, what *is* this? Why do you hate him so much? I can't afford all this ill-feeling.'

'Which I've created, is that it?' She'd almost shouted the words at him.

In the end, they'd smoothed things over and the days had passed pleasantly.

The moment Blaine knocked on her door and she let him into the room, Syrie realised something was wrong.

'I want to talk to you, Syrie.' His eyes went over her.

Her own eyes contained fright. 'What is it? Has Craig collapsed, or something? He has been looking terrible lately.'

'Nothing has happened to him. It's what has happened to you—and what has happened to me, if it comes to that.'

'Would you please get to the point?' Her voice rose.

'Craig has cleared off.'

'Cleared off?' She gave him an amazed stare. 'What are you talking about?'

'Craig has walked out on you. He's stood you up—jilted you . . . take your pick. In other words, he's cleared off to the unknown and, what is more, he appears to have walked out not only on you and on me—but on a mountain of debts,' Blaine informed her brutally.

Syrie felt a rush of heartbeats which nearly suffocated her.

'How do you know?'

'Oh, he left me a most eloquent letter. There's a letter for you too. It was addressed—care of Liselle, who in turn passed it on to me. I should imagine you'd like to read it in private.'

To her horror, Syrie realised Blaine was telling the truth.

'Before I open the letter, tell me what you know.' Her voice was quiet and controlled.

'Well, in the first place he has got himself into a mess with a seedy moneylender who hangs out in a tatty part of Port Louis. It has reached the point where this character has been threatening Craig bodily harm. Apparently, this man was in touch with Craig today. Some time later, Craig had a caller who was sent on behalf of this moneylender. I would go so far as to say that he rough-handled Craig.'

Syrie took a shuddering breath. 'Oh, no! Poor Craig. Why didn't he have the courage to confide in someone? People don't disappear unless they happen to be in great distress. Can't you see that?'

'No, I'm afraid I can't! Craig has taken the easy way out and he's walked out on you—and on me.'

She watched him as he went to the door, and then she lifted the letter from Craig, which he had tossed on a nearby table, and began to open it.

'Syrie, darling,' Craig had written—obviously in great haste. 'I love you, but I've blown it! No matter which way I turn, this man is going to nail me— Blaine will explain who he is. My life is now in grave danger in Mauritius, and I have no option but to get out in a hurry. There is no other way, so try to forgive me. I'll be in touch with you just as soon as I possibly can. I kept borrowing money from Design Dimension which I intended to pay back, without ever having been discovered. I have reason to believe that Blaine had become suspicious, however, and was watching me. The accountants, I found out recently, through Peta, are working on it. Things have become so bad for me that I have begun to function like a mastermind, and so they are in for a hard time trying to unravel this. Believe in me, though, darling. I love you. Craig.'

Blaine returned with two glasses, and he put one of them into her frozen fingers.

'Drink this, Syrie.'

'Do you think a nice strong drink is going to help?' Her voice was bitter.

'Drink the damned stuff. Oh, Syrie . . . ' He heaved a loud sigh. 'What else could you expect? You meet some handsome guy in Greece who sweeps you off your feet.

You go to bed with him and have a whirlwind affair, and then, as if that isn't enough, you virtually hop on the very next plane and fly out to some speck in the Indian Ocean to marry him. Why the hell didn't you listen to me? Why didn't you listen to your innermost self?'

'He was on the verge of marrying me! He wasn't to know this would happen. I thought you liked him? I should have thought you'd be feeling sorry for him right now. He was your best friend, Blaine, or have you forgotten?'

'He wasn't my best friend. He was my partner. I don't have to like him, and I certainly don't have to feel sorry for him after what he's done to me. What is more, neither do you, you little fool.' His blue eyes burned back at her. He lifted his shoulders and took a deep breath. 'Look, if it's any consolation, right at this minute I've also been taken in, but when I look back Craig has always concealed his past. He was always very vague. You'll stay here, of course, under the circumstances. Andy has made all the necessary excuses to everyone. You might like to know that. I think he used a sudden family catastrophe, or something.'

'This is the most bizarre thing I've ever known.' Confused and humiliated she stared back at him. 'I've always considered myself to be capable and competent, and all—all—this—just beats me. I'll stay on in Mauritius, of course. I'll wait for Craig to sort things out. We'll be married later. In the meantime, I'll go ahead and get work, which is what I planned anyway. What is more, I'll start paying you back. I'll even try to sort things out with this moneylender.'

'Don't talk like a fool, Syrie! You'd better get out of that—paraphernalia, and try to—calm down.' His eyes went over her wedding dress.

'I'm very calm,' she lied. He was so callous, she

thought bitterly, feeling the need to break down.

'Would you like me to call my doctor?' Obviously he realised just how brutal he had been. 'Maybe he can prescribe something to make you sleep.'

'I *have* something to make me sleep,' she lied again. 'I'll move out, though. I'll ring the hotel.'

'I've said you're to stay here! Just leave it at that. You can stay here for as long as you want. If it will make you feel better, you can pay for the accommodation.'

She wondered whether he had been aware of the relief which had flooded through her as he made for the door.

After having pretended that she was asleep every time Liselle or Blaine knocked on her door and looked in, she got up in the late afternoon and changed into a thick blue cotton caftan and sandals and made her way downstairs.

The house was very quiet and there was no sign of Blaine. The sun had set, but everything was bathed in a deep orange glow.

On the way to the beach, her caftan brushed the long, slim length of her bare legs, and a breeze blew her tawny hair about her face. Night was falling, she thought. It should have been her wedding night. Depression set upon her like a rock.

She sat down on the sand and drew her knees up to her chin and put her arms around them.

'I've been looking everywhere for you.' Blaine interrupted her thoughts, and she drew a quick breath and looked up at him.

He sat down beside her. 'I should have known you'd be here.' She did not answer and he said, 'Syrie? I've been worried about you.'

'Have you?' Her voice was flat.

'Well, of course!'

After a moment she said, 'I may be depressed, but that doesn't mean I'm going to commit suicide. Did you think

I'd come to drown myself?' Her laugh was soft and bitter.

He shifted position to look at her. 'Cut it out, Syrie, for goodness' sake.'

'You could have helped him. You could have . . . '

'*I* could have? Don't try to shift Craig's guilt on to me, Syrie.'

Some way off, a group of young people had come on to the beach, and within seconds had started to dance the *sega*. Someone had started a fire, and Syrie could see the writhing figures of the dancers as they danced to music made by primitive triangles, maracas, tambourines and a ravane. It was, she thought dismally, a cry from the soul, but no doubt stimulated by local rum. Her control was cracking and she found herself beginning to sob.

Blaine took her into his arms.

'Don't,' she said.

'What's the point of sobbing like this unless you've got a pair of arms to hold you? Keep still, Syrie. I just want to hold you.' He pushed back her hair and tried to look into her face.

'I love him.' She wept uncontrollably.

'You love him?' Blaine's voice was hard now. 'You love him—after what he has done to you? Well, Syrie, I can only attribute that to stark madness.' He stood up abruptly and, reaching down for her wrists, he pulled her up beside him. 'Let's get back to the house. That *sega* is going to turn into a wild binge any moment now.'

'I don't want to go back yet.' Her voice was muffled, and then she caught her breath as he swept her up in his arms and made for the steps leading to the house.

Ignoring her protests, he carried her upstairs to her room and virtually dropped her on to the French four-poster bed.

Looking down at her, he said brutally, 'You'll have to handle this lot on your own, Syrie. I might have offered you my arms on the beach in a weak moment, but I'm damned if I'm going to comfort you now.'

As he went to the door she said, 'Blaine, don't you dare turn this into some freaky farce.'

'That's come from Craig, not me, but I guess you know that.'

Lisellé, her homely face giving nothing away, brought Syrie's breakfast the next morning. After thanking her, Syrie slipped into a satin robe and took the tray out to the long veranda, where she sat in the healing sun.

The marquee and the small dance-floor had been dismantled and were being loaded on to a truck. Another smaller truck stood by—waiting to receive tables and chairs.

Beyond the lagoon, the sea was breathtakingly blue, and the breakers on the reef were sending up cascades of white spray.

Sooner or later, Syrie thought despairingly, she was going to have to face the people who had turned up as guests at the wedding. She was going to have to sort out gifts, and return them along with little notes on flowery notepaper, explaining *why* she was returning them. That was, if Craig did not come back to Mauritius; but she did not want to continue thinking along those lines.

A ripple of fear shot through her when she thought about the moneylender in Port Louis, and she sat for a while, waiting for her nerves to stop shrieking before she went back to her room.

Thirty minutes later, she stepped out of the shower cubicle, and by the time she entered the studio downstairs she looked in complete control, even if she did not feel that way. She immediately came to the conclusion, however, that although it was common knowledge that Craig had gone away no one realised, except Andy and Peta, that he had not been called away to some family crisis, but that he had actually skipped Mauritius. Well, she intended to remain silent on this issue. Not to offer information, she thought dismally, means I am in control.

Tilted back in his chair, Blaine was talking on the phone and, glancing up at Syrie, he gestured to the chair on the other side of his desk. She could see that he was surprised by the fact that she had appeared in the studio as if nothing had happened. She sat down and crossed her legs.

'Blaine,' she said, after he had replaced the receiver, 'may I make an appointment with you for some time today? I have a number of things I would like to discuss with you.'

He shrugged his shoulders. 'My schedule is flexible. How about right now?' Although his voice was hard, she felt the shelter of his nearness, as she had done on previous occasions.

Her eyes met his. 'I want to apply for a position. I have a certain amount of experience. For a while in England I worked for an advertising agency. There must be something I can do here.'

She watched him as he stood up and said, to no one in particular, 'I'll be in the study if anyone wants me and, Peta, fit those slides into a circular tray so that they will be ready to go into the computer this afternoon.'

Peta's eyes flickered from Blaine to Syrie.

'All of them?'

'Yes, all of them.' Blaine started to walk away, but Peta called out.

'What about the one of the girl holding the white poodle with the sparkly rhinestone collar?'

'I've had another look at it. It's OK. Put that one in, too. Come on, Syrie, let's get *something* sorted out for you.' The way in which he said this angered her, but she remained silent.

When they reached the study he asked, 'What can I get you to drink? There should be some fruit juice in the refrigerator.'

Syrie settled herself on one of the high stools.

'Anything cool, Blaine. Pineapple, if you have it, but I'm not fussy.'

She watched him as he moved about the room, looking out tall glasses and filling them with iced pineapple juice.

Passing her a glass, he said, 'We're in luck. Liselle must have put this pineapple juice in here only a few minutes ago.'

The moment he took the stool next to her own, Syrie moved to the sofa. Blaine's blue eyes registered the move. His drink was beside him on the counter. He put one elbow on the counter and she tried to read his feelings, but it was an impossible task.

'I also want to discuss paying you back some—at least some—of the money Craig owes you,' she told him.

'The money Craig *owes* me?' He laughed shortly. 'Well, Syrie, I wouldn't exactly put it that way, but still . . . what Craig—ah—owes this company has nothing whatsoever to do with you. So let's just drop the subject.'

'I don't see why it has nothing to do with me. I am still engaged to him. He has asked me to trust him, which I do, and I intend to go on trusting him. When all this blows over, we are going to be married. That hasn't changed.'

'Well, how you choose to lead your life is your own concern, I suppose, but I have explained the position. Craig was far more crafty than I ever gave him credit for. According to our accountants, he had become quite a mastermind at the game, and let's not tiptoe around the fact that he has helped himself to a considerable amount of money. That still has nothing to do with you, even if you are still engaged to him and choose to go on waiting for a miracle to happen.'

'Blaine, I was hoping to work for Design Dimension, since Craig is—was—your partner. If you're not interested, I'll get work elsewhere. I want to thank you for the offer to go on staying here, but I'll be moving on soon—probably to the hotel near here, if I can get in. You see, I certainly have no intention of skulking back to Athens. In any case, my possessions are already in transit.'

To hide the fact that she was upset, she took a sip of pineapple juice. 'I'll be honest with you,' she went on, after a moment, 'I'm hoping to invest money in Design Dimension—to make up for Craig. I want to help—in fact, I *intend* to help. You can't stop me from doing that. I want to start paying back.'

His electric-blue eyes absorbed her. 'What are you trying to do, Syrie? Step into the role of fairy godmother?' His voice was brutally hard. 'I imagine I can scrape things together, without any help from Craig's devoted fiancée.'

There was a shattered silence on her part, and then she decided to go on.

'Are you interested in having me work for you or not?'

He drained what juice was left in his glass in one gulp. 'I'm thinking about it. Actually, for some time now, I have been thinking of getting rid of Peta.'

Syrie tried not to show her surprise. 'Oh? Why is that?'

'One of my rules is not to allow myself to talk about my employees,' he answered shortly.

'Except your partner? Is that it?' Her eyes were glittering.

'In this case, yes. Except my partner.'

'I suppose you must have your reasons for wanting to get rid of Peta, and if she goes and you took me on, I'd be the new Girl Friday. Is that it?'

He gave her an impatient look. 'Do you think you're too good to be a Girl Friday?'

Feeling her anger building up, she said, 'I didn't say that, did I? You've always got something awful to say. Besides, why don't you try me?'

'I'll think about it,' he answered.

She stood up and put her glass on the smooth golden surface of the counter. 'While you're thinking about it, I'll take myself off for a few days. I just want to get away by myself.'

He stood up suddenly, and she found herself standing very close to him. His eyes held hers.

'Where will you be going?'

'At this stage, I don't really know.' She lifted her shoulders. 'Maybe you could come up with something? Can you recommend a quiet hotel? Not the Bird of Paradise.'

'What do you have in mind? Proximity to the water's edge?' She sensed the cruelty in his voice. 'Something *away* from the sea, on the other hand? Rustic? Tropical? A bungalow complex—but, no you wouldn't want that. Villa—no, I think not . . . '

'Don't mock me, Blaine. You can be so cruel, and the amazing thing is—you aren't even aware of the fact. I won't take up any more of your precious time.'

'Syrie! Just a moment. I'll book you in somewhere. What is more, I'll drive you there to see it. What I have in mind is a small hotel not far from here, but far enough for you to feel alone, since that is what you want. The food's good. Room, with bath. Air-conditioning. It's near the beach, but I should imagine that would be an asset. What is important is the fact that there is no nightlife to speak of. Definitely no *sega* dancing to upset you. You'll be able, in other words, to lick your wounds in peace.'

Angrily, she moved away from him. 'Just cut the sarcasm, Blaine. If you give me the name and telephone number of this hotel, I'll phone myself. I'm not exactly paralysed.'

'The name is Mandelieu, but I'll phone for you. When would you like to book in?'

She made up her mind immediately. 'Today, if possible.'

'I'll see what I can do. About coming to work for us—I feel reasonably sure we can arrange something.'

'Thank you,' she murmured. 'And please at least *consider* my suggestion of having a share in Design Dimension. I want to plan my life.'

He expelled an angry breath. 'You want to plan your life? You know something, Syrie? I lay awake last night, and I though—how could she have been such a little idiot as to give up everything in Athens, and come here to marry a man she hardly knew? How's that for planning, huh? How do you feel now?'

'How do you expect me to feel? I feel bloody awful, if you must know. Nevertheless, I intend staying here. What is more, I intend getting in touch with that moneylender, just to find out what the position is and to try and sort something out with him.'

'Are you out of you mind?' Blaine surveyed her angrily. 'You leave the moneylender alone. This man, from what I know of him, is bad news. What are you trying to do to yourself, Syrie?' He came over to her and took her by the shoulders. 'Under no conceivable circumstances are you to see this character. I forbid it!'

'You forbid it? What right have you to forbid it? And

take your hands off me, Blaine!'

He dropped his arms and drew a breath. 'Let's drop this nonsense.' He glanced at his watch. 'My car's parked at the foot of the steps. I'll meet you there in—say, ten minutes. I'll take you to the hotel and if you like this place you can book in and come back for your clothes and so on. Since you are sticking to Craig, you might as well take advantage of the fact that he left his very nice car parked in one of the garages at the back.'

On the way to the hotel later, she brooded silently, since Blaine made no attempt to involve her in conversation. Eventually, unable to bear the silence another moment, she turned to look at him.

'I fine it absolutely amazing that you didn't sense something was wrong in Craig's life before he got himself into such difficulties. Couldn't you have stopped him? Helped him?' She wanted to lash out at him. 'In a way, I blame you for a lot.'

Blaine swung round in his seat with an expression of anger. 'So, you blame me for a lot? If I were you, Syrie, I'd keep my mouth zipped up. Don't blame me for what Craig's done. When I come to think of it now, all Craig ever thought of was money. Money—when he had it. Money—when he didn't have it. Money—when he wanted it, which was just about all the time. Money—when he craved to spend it. His *whole* life seemed to revolve around money and . . . ' He broke off.

'Money—and—what?' she asked in a brittle voice.

'Oh, forget it,' he snapped. 'I don't want to talk about this guy.'

'In that case, why did you approve of him as a partner?' Syrie's green eyes were furious and hurt.

After a moment he said quietly, 'I had known Craig for some time. I knew he was familiar with the kind of work we do. He was working in Curepipe. He had good references and I had no reason not to trust him. He was more than keen to come into the business.'

'It didn't take you long to change your tune about him, though, did it? You haven't said one decent thing about Craig since he found himself in all this trouble.' Now that she had started, she couldn't stop.

'*Found* himself in trouble?' Blaine laughed outright, but there was nothing attractive in the sound. 'So, Craig just woke up on his wedding day and *found* himself in trouble? Ah, Syrie. You may have worked in London, Amsterdam, Paris, Rome . . . but you have a hell of a lot to find out about men—about life, for that matter. Still, it's taken a flight to Mauritius to find out a few things and to take a few hard knocks. For the record, however, I had nothing to do with Craig's downfall, whether you choose to believe it, or not.'

Syrie turned her face away and bit her lip. She found she was shaking and decided to keep quiet.

The hotel was everything he'd said it was and, just looking at it from the outside, she decided there and then to book in for one week, on the off chance that, if she wanted to stay on, she would have no trouble in doing so.

Blaine went with her to see the room, which had a tropical atmosphere, accentuated by the usual leaning palms, a white beach and blue sea. She asked the young Creole man who had taken them along to the room, for time to decide, and he went back to reception.

Syrie's eyes went immediately to the double bed with its curved wicker bedhead and attractive fringed cover, which resembled a pastel-shaded oriental rug. Two wicker chairs stood beside a round table which had a floor-length cloth. There were potted palms reaching almost to the ceiling, amber bedside lights on low wicker chests, and sliding glass doors opened to a small private patio. The adjoining bathroom had amber tiles and was also well-stocked with greenery.

'Thank you for bringing me here,' she said, looking at Blaine's hard face. 'It's just what I had hoped for.'

'Good.' He inclined his head. 'If ever you want me—just lift the phone and I'll be over.'

'I'll be OK. You might have to get in touch with me if you hear anything, of course.'

'What do you expect me to hear, Syrie? That all is well? Everything has blown over? That a miracle has happened? That the moneylender and Design Dimension have been paid back in full, plus interest?'

'I mean, if there is something I should know about. There might be a letter for me in the near future—while I am here, in other words. If you phone me, I'll drive over in Craig's car and collect it.'

This was another thing which puzzled her. Since Craig had left the car behind, she had often wondered how he had got to the airport, for he must have flown out of Mauritius. The answer seemed clear enough. Peta must have taken him to the airport in her car.

'This self-sacrificing role you have adopted astounds me,' Blaine was saying. 'Don't let him do this to you.' There was a savage edge to his voice.

'I have not *adopted* a self-sacrificing role. This is not a role! I love him.'

'You love him and you blame me, is that it? It defeats me why you should be blaming me for any of this. Let's go. I've got work to do.' Anger made his voice harsh. 'Anyway, this is as good a place as any to hole up in.'

'Damn you, Blaine! I merely wish to think in an impersonal environment.'

'Well, you've got a lot of thinking to do, and I'm merely breaking it gently. But on the other hand, you never know . . . ' he drawled the last two words, 'your fiancé might just turn out to be tops.' He spread his palms. 'I mean, who's to tell?'

'I don't need your smart dialogue, Blaine. I'll take Craig just the way he is. I'm prepared to take the good times *and* the bad times. Just remember that, will you, when you're baiting me?'

They did not talk going back to his house, but before she went up to her room to pack a few clothes she said, 'Thank you for taking me to the hotel. Don't let's quarrel, Blaine. *Please.* Why are you going on like this?'

'I'm sure you can work that out for yourself. You know where to find me, Syrie . . . '

CHAPTER SIX

SYRIE sipped a daiquiri cocktail, and from the small, private patio in front of her room she gazed at the sea.

The Hotel Mandelieu appeared to be quite full, but there were not enough guests to get worked up about.

Dinner was a buffet-style affair and she smiled politely at people but, when it came to talking about herself, she was politely evasive. She remembered reading somewhere that to be glamorous a woman had to be absolutely mysterious about the past, and so mysterious she would be. Meeting people who had been at the party in Blaine's house and who had sent wedding gifts was going to be another matter, however, but she would deal with that when the time came.

She spent the next few days sunbathing on the beach, where she appeared relaxed and glamorous. Inwardly, though, she was worried about Craig—wherever he was. Several times she wrote him letters which expressed her love and concern for him, and which, of course, she could not post. During fits of anger at what he had done to her, she wrote long, spiteful and vicious letters, and had no option but to tear them up, too.

Eventually, after hours of sunbathing, swimming, eating, walking and even taking long, useless baths in her bedroom, which resembled a jungle, she decided to drive to Port Louis to see the moneylender and to try to reason with him and reach some arrangement, whereby it would be safe for Craig to return to Mauritius and start getting his life—and hers—together again.

On an impulse, she picked up the phone and began to

dial.

Peta Faber answered. 'Design Dimension. Can I be of assistance?'

'Blaine Cartwright, please.' At the sound of this insolent girl's voice, Syrie tried to control her angry breathing.

'Who is it?'

'Never mind who it is—just put me on to Blaine.'

A moment later, Blaine was saying impatiently, 'What is it, Syrie?'

He might have shown concern instead of impatience, she thought resentfully. What was more, Peta had known who was calling, without having to ask.

'It's about that moneylender. I should imagine you know his name and whereabouts. I want to get in touch with him to try and sort something out with him.'

There was a long silence and she broke it.

'Blaine? Are you there?'

'No. I've just taken off to the moon! I can't get over you, do you know that? You seem hell-bent on a path to self-destruction, don't you? You don't stop to think. I've told you, you're not to see this man. He's dangerous. What the hell has all this got to do with you, anyway, since Craig saw fit to jilt you? That has a nice old-fashioned ring to it, hasn't it? But, there's nothing deserving respect about capriciously casting off a girl on her wedding day, is there?'

Syrie was off the bed now, where she had been sitting, and she stood restlessly next to the wicker chest on which the phone rested.

'You have no right to bully me like this. I merely phoned for information.'

'Just a moment, Syrie. Andy, the visuals are ready.'

Patiently, Syrie waited for Blaine to finish his conversation with Andy at the other end, and then he was back on the line again.

'OK, Syrie . . . where were we? Ah, yes . . . what we have here is one very dangerous character.'

'I'm not denying that, but all I need from you, Blaine, is his name and address, if you have that. And, while we're having this discussion, I'd also like a statement of what Craig owes you, just as soon as you are in a position to let me have one.' She took a breath. 'I didn't phone to ask for your opinion. I'm simply not interested in it.'

'Don't be sarcastic with me,' he answered back sharply. 'I'm very busy right now as it is, without you bothering me. I'm not in a particularly good mood, what is more.'

'Oh! Well, that's a pity about you—and just for the record, for what it's worth, that makes two of us. I'm not in a very good mood, either. I wouldn't be phoning otherwise. Can't you try to understand what's going on here? It's essential for me to start working things out in Craig's interest, since he has had to run for his very life. I can at least try to reason with this man in Port Louis. I might be able to show him that Craig is as anxious as I am to start paying back, no matter how slowly at first.'

'You are not responsible for *any* of this guy's debts, except for those debts which you might have helped him to incur. That's up to you, but . . . just a moment . . . Yes, what is it now?'

Syrie could hear Peta's strident voice in the background, and then Blaine was saying, 'Well, where are the colour proofs? What do you mean, you don't know?'

In a fit of rage, Syrie slammed down the receiver and went towards the sliding doors and then out to the lawn.

Thanks, she thought bitterly. I'm sorry I interrupted your busy day, Blaine Cartwright. Oh, Craig . . . what have you done to me? Her nerves were at screaming point.

Since she had intended going to Port Louis, she was wearing pale blue jeans and a white silk shirt. A silver and turquoise belt hung loosely at her waist, and a matching bracelet looked good on her tanned wrist.

She took the flagstone path to the beach and, slipping off the sandals she was wearing, she felt the soft powdery sand caressing her skin. Her tawny hair, attractively streaked from long hours in the sun, touched the delicate line of her jaw.

She should have been on her honeymoon, she thought bitterly, looking at her long oval nails, which were varnished a delicate pink. She and Craig should have been exploring the island of Réunion, where the volcano was still active.

After walking for a while, she turned back and had just reached the vicinity of the hotel when she saw Blaine striding through the sand towards her. She stared at him angrily.

His blue eyes clashed with her. 'So you resorted to that old feminine trick of hanging up on me?'

'What are you doing here, anyway? I thought you were *so busy*?' Her voice was thick with sarcasm.

'Well, let's put it this way—you put an end to all that.'

'Oh, I see. What I wanted from you, Blaine, was the address of the man. If you have it, which I feel you do, it wouldn't have taken five minutes of your valuable time.'

'I don't have it. Even if I did, I wouldn't give it to you. What kind of damn fool do you take me for? You keep out of this.'

'But don't you see? If he thinks I am concerned, he might . . . '

'He might—what? *If* he sees you're concerned!' His blue eyes were blazing now. 'With you, it's a case of if, if, if. Look, you'd better make up your mind that this man is not worried whether you are concerned or not. In fact, Syrie from Athens, he doesn't give a Continental Damn, in capital letters, what you think. His only concern is for himself and the money which is owing to him. Just try to get that into your head. Another thing, if he gets in touch with you, and I've said *if*—I want you to let me know about it immediately.'

'Why should I? This has nothing to do with you—except that you probably helped to get Craig's back to the wall with your demands of more and more money for your precious business.'

'You want to watch that tongue of yours.' Blaine was furious now. 'It could get you into a lot of trouble. I have been trying to get across to you, however, that this man in Port Louis has been threatening Craig to such an extent that Craig cleared off. This moneylender is not a moneylender because he is chicken-hearted, dear girl . . . '

'What about the police?' she asked. 'Or don't police exist in Mauritius? In any case, I'll manage things my way. I don't intend just rushing into things. I'll feel my way first. I'm a very disciplined person.' She looked down and began turning her turquoise and silver bracelet.

'Yeah, it certainly looks like it.' Blaine's voice was scathing. 'In fact, you're *so disciplined*—that's why you're here, isn't it? And talking about "feeling your way"—just be careful this man doesn't end up feeling you instead.'

'Don't you dare talk to me like that, Blaine! I don't regret coming to Mauritius,' she told him, regretting it very much at this moment. 'What is more, I intend staying here and sorting things out. I wonder what you'll have to say when Craig comes back one day?'

'I think you've lost sight of the future. He's not coming back. What's there to come back to when he believes he can get you to go to him, complete with your inheritance?'

'Both ways—I trust him, and my inheritance has nothing to do with it.'

'You really believe that, huh?' Blaine shook his head. 'Syrie, your faith in Craig is difficult to understand.'

She turned round to look at the sea and then she swung round again, facing him. 'Would you mind getting off this beach? I don't want you here. I find you offensive.'

'You're being hoodwinked by a common thief, Syrie. A liar and a thief!'

'You heartless devil!'

There was a sudden charged silence and then, still holding her wrist, Blaine pulled her towards him until his thighs were pressed against her own. His kiss was long and disturbing, deepening threateningly, as he tightened his hold on her waist. He moved his hands to her hips and then went on kissing her, almost kneading her into him. She found herself sinking into a fantasy of making love with him, and she found herself thinking, in a haze of almost terrifying sensations, that Craig had never had the power to thrill her to this extent.

When she was least expecting it, Blaine released her.

'You'd better start thinking,' he told her, 'about *us*—but I told you that at the airport, didn't I?'

'What are you expecting, Blaine, now that Craig *appears* to be out of the picture? That I turn myself over to you?'

'Right from the word go, Craig had no right to involve you in the rubble of his life,' he answered.

'Well, I am involved. I was on the point of marrying him, if some crook hadn't intervened.'

'And it would have taken no more than five minutes, the way he had planned things. Your marriage vows would have taken no more than a few minutes, but he would have hooked you, along with everything he thinks you own. I've already told you that—drink always loosened Craig's tongue.'

'I don't believe you. You're a liar, Blaine!'

He went on brutally, 'You jumped into bed with a guy who was on holiday in Athens, and after giving up everything there—your job, your apartment, your car—you fly out here and expect to live happily ever after.'

'It wasn't like that, blast you! I didn't just jump into bed with him in Athens. Are you enjoying all this? Because if you are, I'm not.'

Blaine stared at her for a long moment before he said softly, 'You'll be late for another nice long walk along the beach. Is this all you have to live for? The memory of Craig and this crazy idea you have of getting his life back into some kind of order? Good luck to you, Syrie.' He turned and left her; frustrated and furious, she watched him as he made his way towards the path.

She went back to the hotel and, soon after entering her room, the phone rang and she picked it up, half expecting to hear Blaine's voice. Instead, it was Peta Faber.

'You might as well be aware of it, I know what's going on around here, and I agree—you should help Craig.'

'Why do you agree?' Syrie's voice was hard.

'Well, you want him back, don't you?'

'Yes, and so do you. Right?' The moment she uttered the words, Syrie felt she had betrayed Craig. He had explained about Peta and she had squashed what doubts she'd harboured and was on the point of marrying him when disaster had struck—so why change now?

'Do you want me to put this phone down?' Peta asked. 'If so, just say the word.'

'Naturally, now that you've got this far, I don't want you to put the phone down. Where are you phoning from, Peta? Surely not the studio?'

'Of course not the studio. What do you take me for? I'm phoning from Craig's chalet. The new people haven't moved in yet. I have my own key.'

Syrie felt the fine gold hairs on her arms beginning to bristle.

'I'll get my pen,' she said, and a moment later Peta gave her the address of the moneylender in Port Louis.

'His name is Jubala Jurrah.'

'Are you sure?' Syrie asked.

'Of course I'm sure. The address is sixty-seven, Banane Lane, off Cemetery Road. Have you got that? Don't tell Blaine I told you, by the way.' Peta rang off.

Although she was tense after receiving this information, Syrie dialled the number a few minutes later and asked to speak to Monsieur Jurrah.

'Please state your interest in *monsieur*.' The answer came back in French, and Syrie answered in the same language.

After a short silence she was told that *monsieur* would see her tomorrow morning at ten o'clock—and that was that, thought Syrie—beginning to shake.

Since she had not been to Port Louis, she went along to reception and helped herself to available information on the island of Mauritius, along with a map especially for tourists.

Port Louis, she discovered the following day, was a bustling, haphazard muddle of buildings, streets and alley-ways. The narrow basalt sidewalks were crammed with Indian women wearing the most gorgeous saris, Creole girls clad in vivid cottons, Chinese men in narrow trousers and shirts, and Moslems with goatee beards and wearing tarbooshes. There were stores and market-places, along with faded houses, with balconies and jalousies. Towering above the harbour were the sentinels of the Moka range.

In Port Louis, she discovered, pedestrians threatened to get tangled up in the traffic, which also involved darting pigs, piglets and chickens. One wrong turn caused her to miss Cemetery Road and, in turn, Banane Lane.

She was about to give up on number sixty-seven when she saw a sign which hung at an angle of forty-five degrees and looked as though it had endured many cyclones.

The sagging double-storey stood next to a tobacconist shop named *Blague à Tabac*, and an outsize tobacco pouch swayed from a metal rod.

She parked the car and gazed at the house with its fretted balcony and peeling wooden jalousies over the windows. Heat shimmered on the narrow lane.

Most of the seats in the waiting-room were taken and, feeling all eyes on her, she approached the dark girl at the desk.

'I have an appointment,' she said in French, 'with Monsieur Jurrah at ten o'clock. The name is Mademoiselle Knight.'

'Please take a seat.'

Looking casually chic, Syrie chose a chair and sat down. She crossed her legs and kept her eyes on the toe of one inky-blue court shoe. After several moments, during which she suddenly seemed to be developing tachycardia, she lifted her lashes and surveyed the unwelcoming room and its occupants. It was hard to think of tall, handsome Craig sitting here, as he must have done, as he came to arrange for money with which to pay his debts.

The waiting-room was furnished in brown and the upholstery of the chair on which she was sitting, made her feel that she was perched on a tatty, greasy old teddy-bear. Everything smelled of stale cigarette smoke, like the casino of some dive, and everything was worn. Overhead, the blades of a fan turned lethargically, only just stirring the air and no more.

Finally her name was called and she followed the girl into the office of Monsieur Jubala Jurrah, who rose slightly and then waved a plump hand in the direction of the chair opposite his. Syrie was aware of the rhythmic whirr of yet another ceiling fan.

'*Monsieur*,' her wide green eyes met his small black ones across the brown desk, 'may we conduct this interview in English?' She took a little breath. '*Parlez-vous Anglais?*'

'Certainly, *mademoiselle*.' Bland-faced and inscrutable, Jurrah was a large man with heavily lidded black eyes, which appeared to be half closed most of the time. His hair was inclined to be wispy, but it was very black, and it curled over his collar. Syrie noticed the centre parting, for some reason or another. His narrow moustache and beard were both well-trimmed, and the beard just cupped his chin.

Suddenly he smiled and she felt, foolishly she knew, that this man could be capable of both surprising tenderness—and cruelty. She could imagine him stroking a tiny kitten, or smoothing the brow of a sick grandchild. She could also imagine him having someone murdered—on his behalf—a man, or even a woman, in cold blood. His smile vanished as quickly as it had come.

Syrie said, 'Let's get straight to the point, *monsieur*. I have not come here to borrow money, I have . . . '

He interrupted her quickly. 'I already know about

you, *mademoiselle*. Your husband-to-be spoke of you, of
course.' He seemed not to speak the words, but to drawl
them.

'What did he tell you about me?' Her voice was cold.

'That you were arriving from Athens and were to be
married on our little island.' He smiled again, but the
smile did not reach his eyes. 'He explained that once you
arrived here you would be in a position to help him, in
the very near future—financially, that is. In other words,
mademoiselle, he spoke of your inheritance. What else?'
He had a way of tilting his head back and looking at her
with almost closed eyes. He almost appeared to be in
pain.

'Do you know, Monsieur Jurrah, that by threatening
Craig Knox you have smashed our plans? We should
have been married by now. I have come here to try and
make you see reason and to try and sort something out
with you.'

He laughed at that. Syrie felt suddenly sick.

'This man Knox, as you know—just as I know you
never *did* get to marry him—is in debt to me. You would
not be here, otherwise—no?' He patted a folder which
was on the desk in front of him. 'I have drawn up the
figures for you to scrutinise, *mademoiselle*. They are for
you to examine when you get back home, and which we
will discuss on your next visit.'

Seated opposite him, Syrie had the unsettling and
frightening sensation that a very large hooded cobra was
about to lunge at her and strike. She also realised that
this man was 'feeling his way with her' just as she had
intended to do just that—with him. She also realised
that, now she had come to him, he was going to work on
her until she ended by paying him whatever she could.
At the time of mentioning her inheritance to Craig,
she'd had no idea that this would be the outcome.

Jubala Jurrah's smooth voice interrupted her. 'Maybe you have an idea where he has fled to?'

'I have no idea, *monsieur*.'

'At a guess, maybe?' There was a note of seduction, almost. 'Come, *mademoiselle*—at a guess.'

'I couldn't begin to guess. For all I know, he might have gone to Australia.' Now why had she said that? Why had she said anything? She could have kicked herself.

'But you mention Australia. Why?'

'For no good reason. I mentioned it as one would mention Timbuktu, for instance.'

'Timbuktu?' He was beginning to sound angry. 'You are being sarcastic, I think?'

'Monsieur Jurrah, I was thinking of the Australian outback—you know—somewhere remote. Hard to find. I don't know where he has gone to.' They exchanged a look of pure dislike, and she shivered.

He slid the folder across the brown expanse of his desk. 'Take this with you. Examine it. Make an appointment for a week today. My secretary will arrange it. After all, this is what you came here for—to find out for yourself and to try and sort something out with me, was it not?'

'I came out of common decency,' she replied.

'Common decency does not concern me, *mademoiselle*. If I had to rely on this, I would be in queer street, as I believe it is known.'

The fact that Craig had mentioned her inheritance to this man sickened her and left her feeling outraged.

'I'm surprised you didn't go to the police,' she said sarcastically, knowing full well that a man like this would not go to the police. He would sort things out in his own violent way.

'Well, be thankful for small mercies, I did not. So why not make the most of it? A week from today, *mademoiselle*.' He swung round in his swivel chair, thus turning his back on her. He peaked his fingers and Syrie could hear him humming.

She left without glancing at the receptionist and went out to the lane, off Cemetery Road. A scattering of wind-battered banana trees grew in clusters on either side of the lane. Some of them had puny hands of finger-shaped fruit, and their yellow skins were pock-marked with brown.

The houses in the area were run-down, but something told her that Jubala Jurrah would live elsewhere in luxury.

By the time she got back to the Hotel Mandelieu, she had a splitting headache and, after taking something to relieve the pain, she lay down and closed her eyes. A huge wave of depression exploded over her.

Later, she converted the money Craig owed Jubala Jurrah to the British pound and nearly fainted when she realised that he owed the moneylender roughly thirty thousand pounds.

Poor Craig! She found herself crying for him.

After a while she ran a bath. After all she had been through, it was wonderfully soothing to stretch back in the warm, scented water.

Later, because she knew she'd have to eat, even if she did not feel that she could at this moment, she looked out a two-tiered white skirt and a long sleeveless top.

Jubala Jurrah's green folder lay on the round skirted table, where she had tossed it in her moment of despair. Just looking at it made her feel sick.

There was a knock on the door and she went to open it. Blaine was standing there, and his blue eyes went right over her.

'Are you going out?'

'No.' She wanted to tell him how pleased she was to see him—just standing there—but she went on, 'Who would I be going out with?'

'How the devil should I know?' His voice was curt. 'Are you going to keep me standing here, or am I going to be invited to step inside?'

Her brain seemed to have stopped working, and then she moved so that he might enter the room. There was a flurry of flounces as she closed the door and went to stand a little way from him.

'So, Syrie, how did you spend the day?' His eyes held hers.

'I just *spent* the day. That's all.'

'Nothing else? Nothing interesting?'

She watched him as he went over to the round table. He sat down on one of the wicker chairs and crossed one leg over the thigh of the other.

'Since you are so inquisitive, I spent it with a multi-millionaire.'

His blue eyes flickered over the green folder.

'I'm tempted to throttle you,' he said.

'Just try,' she retorted.

'You've been to see Jubala Jurrah, right? How did you find out where to find this individual?'

'I don't want to talk about it.'

'No? I'm sure you don't. You're a fast worker. You didn't waste time in getting to work on Peta, did you?'

'What makes you think I've been to work on Peta?' she asked angrily.'

'It figures. If anybody would know, she would, and I guess I don't have to explain why.'

Syrie crossed over to the bed and sat down on the edge of it.

'Since when do I have to seek your approval before I do anything? I've been "doing my own thing" for years, and I'm certainly not going to stop now. I'm quite capable of conducting my own affairs, in other words.'

'Go on.' His eyes had a cynical glint to them. 'You interest me. You really do. One day you're going to bite off more than you can chew. There was no need for you to go and see this corrupt moneylender. I've told you, repeatedly, he's a dangerous customer. Why can't you listen to me? You know as well as I do that you are not answerable for the debts which have been incurred by Craig Knox—especially as he didn't get round to marrying you. He cleared off without giving you a damned thought.' His eyes went back to the folder. 'How much does he owe this man, by the way?'

'It's a lot of money, and I don't intend to disclose the amount to you. This involves Craig, Jubala Jurrah—and me.'

'And you?' His voice was scathing. '*I* see . . . And now that you have involved yourself, what do you intend to do about it?'

'I haven't thought about it.'

'Well, you'd better *start* thinking, now that you have set the ball rolling. Don't you see how serious this is? Jurrah is a man who would stop at nothing. He has a scheming brain, but I guess you found that out for yourself. He also has a tendency, I've been told, to resort to violence when he wants to know something. He boasts of running his own "little Mafia" in Mauritius.'

'Don't try to scare me, Blaine.' She took a breath. 'There is nothing he can do to me.'

When Blaine was angry, she thought, he seemed to exude animal magnetism.

'I'll tell you something else, Syrie,' he was saying. 'You seem to have a built-in talent for complicating your life; the first complication being the big romance of the century. Maybe now you'll begin to realise that Craig had calculated that in the near future your inheritance would be his. *He saw it that way.* He knew you would help him.'

Her eyes widened when he picked up the papers which had been in the folder and which he had taken out while he was talking to her, and tore them in pieces.

'I'll take care of this rat. You are to have nothing more to do with him. Is that clear, or do I have to shake some sense into you?'

He stood up, came over to her and took her by the shoulders. As she stared back at him, she accepted the force of the attraction he held for her and which she had been aware of at the airport.

'Why add Jurrah to the list of your trials and tribulations?'

When he released her he picked up the large envelope which he had been carrying when he'd arrived, and which he had tossed on to the bed.

'Here!' he said violently. 'These are the photographs taken on the night of the party. They arrived at my place today, and since the party was held there, my address appeared on the envelope. Let's hope they cheer you up.'

Syrie watched him go, and she listened to the door as he banged it shut.

Later on, when she could bring herself to do it, she looked at the photographs and she noticed how devoid Craig's face was of any emotion.

CHAPTER SEVEN

THREE days later, while writing a letter in her room at the hotel, Syrie received a phone call from Jubala Jurrah. The fact that he'd found out where to find her chilled her.

'I find it regrettable, *mademoiselle*,' he said, 'that you have thought fit to involve Monsieur Cartwright in our affairs. He has been into my office, and the way in which he thought fit to threaten me has angered me. My fight is, after all, with your fiancé and not his partner. Since, however, your fiancé has thought fit to leave this country, I feel it is only right that you should keep in touch with me and inform me of his whereabouts, so that an understanding can be reached. You were supposed to have made an appointment with my secretary, or had you forgotten?'

Syrie experienced a quick surge of relief to hear that Blaine had taken it upon himself to step in, but she knew that he would not have given Jurrah her hotel telephone number, and this added to her fear of the man.

'You will have a long wait, Monsieur Jurrah. I have no intention of making another appointment, unless, of course, you are willing to show leniency towards my fiancé.' She replaced the receiver immediately and her heart was beating heavily. On an impulse, she lifted he phone again and asked for room service.

A few minutes later, she was sipping a Scotch and soda in an effort to calm her nerves.

She had been writing to her aunt in England, explaining that, due to illness in the Knox family, Craig

121

had gone to Australia and that the wedding had been postponed at the very last moment. 'We'll look forward to you both visiting us, directly Uncle Simon is fit enough to travel,' she'd written, 'and, of course, when Craig gets back to Mauritius.'

Putting her glass down, she stood up and went to the skirted table. Tearing the letter to shreds, she dropped the pieces into the waste-paper basket. How *can* Craig come back? she asked herself. How? Despair settled over her.

After a restless night, she was still in bed when the phone rang, and a moment later her nerves jumped at the sound of Blaine's voice.

'What are you doing?' he asked.

'I'm still in bed.'

'Still in bed—at this hour? Syrie, when are you going to get your act together? Isn't it about time you came to terms with life?'

'Actually, I've never lost terms with life. I've been taking a rest. In fact, I'll be leaving the hotel soon.'

'And then?'

After a moment she said, 'Just say the word and I'll report for work.'

'In that case we'll talk. I'll expect you here within an hour.' He rang off without waiting on her reply.

When she walked into the studio later, she was wearing a long white jacket, printed with thick golden-brown wavy stripes, a golden-brown camisole top and skirt. The skirt flared from her hips in a swirl of soft pleats, and a gold belt emphasised her slim waist. She looked sleekly fashionable and she knew it. Blaine's blue eyes went over her.

'So?' He stood up. 'Let's get something sorted out. We'll go along to the study, where we can talk in peace and have some fruit juice.'

A few moments later he was passing her a glass of

mango juice.

'I must say, you're looking very thin—you've lost weight—very streaky,' his eyes went to her sun-streaked tawny hair, 'and very golden.' He lifted his tall glass to his lips. 'Cheers! By the way, you do drink mango juice, I take it?'

'As you see . . .' She tried to keep her eyes from going over *him* but, at a brief glance as she'd entered the studio, she'd noticed his white trousers and dark blue T-shirt. He was tanned and he glowed with perfect health. He'd make a wonderful lover, she found herself thinking. What was more—a wonderful—if bossy—husband.

Impatiently, he broke into her thoughts. 'Are you listening to me?'

'Yes.'

'What did I just say?'

'You *just* said you'd been re-shuffling the staff.'

The smile, showing the groove in his tanned cheek, was sarcastic. 'I'm surprised you knew. To continue . . . I am also in the process of taking on a new man. Peta, you might have noticed, has now left us.'

'I had noticed,' Syrie murmured, 'that she wasn't in the studio.'

Blaine went on, 'Her work left a lot to be desired, apart from the fact that she was unpopular. She was Craig's choice.'

'Where has she gone?' Syrie asked.

'She has gone back to work for a pharmacist in Curepipe, where she had a job selling films. That is where Craig picked her up.'

What followed could not exactly be termed as a business conference, but at the end of their discussion Blaine said, 'Well, Syrie, this calls for our first business luncheon. What do you say?'

She stood up. 'You have gone to considerable length

to explain that I'll be working for Design Dimension, but you have said nothing about my wanting to inject money into the business in the near futue, resulting in a share.'

'I don't want your money,' he answered curtly. 'I thought I'd made that clear.'

'I don't seem to be able to get anywhere with you. In the meantime, Blaine, I will go ahead and open a special account, and the money will go towards paying back at least some of the money which Craig—took. Borrowed. You can't stop me from doing that, whether I work for you or for someone else.'

'You can open as many bank accounts as you like, but I don't want to hear about it. Save the money for a rainy day, when your lover might send for it.'

Boiling with temper, she allowed that remark to slide.

They were in the big entrance hall when Blaine said casually, 'Your room has been prepared for you. You might as well stay here, since you will be working here.'

She realised how vulnerable she was. 'I hadn't thought about where I'm going to stay.'

'Well, I had. You'll stay here. That, to me, makes sense.' Their eyes met.

'Eventually, I'll be moving to the chalet Craig and I decided on. There's a bit of a hassle going on there. The people have not yet moved out and they keep asking for more time.'

'In that case, everything is settled.' He glanced at his watch. 'Perhaps you'd like to go upstairs while I attend to something in the studio, and then we'll go to lunch.' His voice carried a note of authority which, strangely enough, she welcomed at this particular time of her life.

Liselle was in the wide corridor upstairs, and when she saw Syrie she said, 'There was no mail to forward to your hotel, *mademoiselle*—as you requested. There was, however, a phone call. I gave the gentleman your hotel number.'

Syrie's heart skipped a beat. The 'gentleman' would have been Jubala Jurrah, of course.

The room brought back painful memories. Memories of the day when she had arrived on the island to marry Craig and Blaine had brought her here. Memories of what should have been her wedding day. Looking round, she knew that she had to face up to the situation as unemotionally as possible, unless she decided to live somewhere else.

She combed her hair and touched up her make-up, and then went downstairs and outside to the long veranda, where she sat in a comfortable wicker chair to wait for Blaine. From the hall, he would be sure to see her. It was difficult to believe that only two weeks ago a huge marquee to accommodate wedding guests had stood on the lawn in front of her. At the time, she had insisted on paying many of the accounts involved in the forthcoming reception and, what was more, she had felt good about helping Craig. What it had really amounted to was that she was merely playing her part.

More and more accounts had come in; many of them having nothing to do with the wedding-to-be. She realised that she had a lot of things to face up to. For one thing, Craig had suggested they open a store account in her name but which they could *both* use. The object of the account was mainly for use when it came to purchasing items for the new chalet, but she had made the discovery that Craig had been buying at random. And yet, looking back, he'd seemed to have nothing to show from these shopping expeditions on his own.

Blaine interrupted her morbid thoughts, and she reached for her peach-coloured bag which went so well with the golden-brown and white outfit with its thin gold belt.

His blue eyes met hers. 'OK? Let's go, then.'

She felt the attraction he'd always held for her—from the moment she'd seen him striding towards her at Plaisance Airport. Why couldn't it have been Blaine holidaying in Greece?

'We're going to Curepipe,' Blaine was saying.

'That sounds nice.' She kept her voice neutral.

They did not talk much on the way. Blaine drove well, and she found herself relaxing for the first time in weeks.

As they drove into Curepipe she said, 'It was quite a long way to come, Blaine.'

'But worth it, I hope.' He smiled at her. 'Besides, there's no hurry to get back.'

As they walked in the direction of the restaurant, her eyes scanned the shops and she noticed the wide range of oriental and western merchandise, and a variety of traditional craft products including articles made of tortoiseshell, jade, ivory, seashells and leather. There was a lot of exciting basket-work, Indian jewellery, Mauritian pottery and Chinese embroideries, silks and rolls of brightly coloured materials. Most of the shops had such fascinating names as City of Peking, Oriental Bazaar and the Silk Dragon, and there were goods from China, Hong Kong, Japan, Thailand, the Philippines and Indonesia.

Syrie realised, suddenly, that she should have seen all this with Craig after their honeymoon, when they were settled in Mauritius, and she felt utterly depressed.

'Would you like to shop after lunch?' Blaine asked.

Hiding her misery, she said, 'I'd love to.'

The restaurant was very French and had a vast stone fireplace at one end, and interesting pieces of gleaming copper.

She and Blaine were asked to sit at the small bar until

their order had been taken and the food prepared for them.

Womanlike, Syrie wanted to talk about Craig—at the risk of causing 'feeling'. Perhaps, she asked herself, this was exactly what she wanted?

'Blaine,' she said, 'did you know that Craig had been married before?' This was something she'd made up her mind to forget about from the moment Craig had told her. He had been quite honest with her, and for this reason alone she felt she should go on believing in him. After all, he could have kept this bit of news from her.

'No.' Blaine's voice was curt. 'I'm not surprised to hear it, though. What happened to the marriage? Wasn't she able to *understand* him?'

'Don't be sarcastic.' She took an angry breath. 'As far as I know, she's still in New Zealand.'

'But Craig came from Australia.' There was interest in Blaine's voice now.

As soon as he had spoken, she felt a cold shiver go right through her. Australia! She thought of what she'd so carelessly said to Jubala Jurrah.

'No, you're wrong about that. Craig came from New Zealand,' she said quickly.

'Did you agree to have lunch with me so that you could do a little belated research on the man who callously walked out on you?' Blaine's mood was changing drastically.

Syrie's green eyes accused him. 'You did know, didn't you?'

'What difference does it make? Besides, you should have done your research before you came flying out here to marry him.'

'Thank you.' She took a sip of her drink and shuddered a little at its strength. What on earth had she ordered? Something with a fancy name, just to irritate

Blaine, no doubt. 'You're so brutal, Blaine. I didn't need to do research, as you put it. I fell in love with Craig.'

His sarcastic reply really rattled her. 'What is so bloody unfathomable is that you profess to be still in love with him. You're a glutton for punishment, aren't you?'

That's nonsense. I love him—*and* I trust him.'

Blaine lifted his glass in mock toast. 'And, I admire your touching blind trust. Too bad he's not here to witness it.'

Every stool in the small bar off the restaurant was occupied now, as more and more people arrived for lunch. Syrie and Blaine were crushed together, so that their knees were touching. She felt the warmth of his, and was aware of the masculine and disturbingly familiar scent of him.

'I'm without the man I love and was supposed to have married, whereas all that's happened to you is you're without your partner.' She exuded hostility and, what was more, she found she couldn't help it. Maybe it was the cocktail. Or maybe it was that she wished to goad Blaine.

He exuded hostility back. 'I'm a lucky man, aren't I?'

'Even then,' her voice rose a little, 'you're not losing any time, are you? You've already—ah—been to work on me, and you've already got a new partner lined up.'

'I was honest. I got to work on you, as you put it, the moment I saw you at the airport. I didn't wait until *after* he'd skipped the country. There's nothing dishonest about me.'

'What was so honest about making a pass at your partner's fiancée while he happened to be away in Réunion?'

'*With* his girlfriend—and do you have to let the whole restaurant in on this?' Blaine's angry eyes met hers.

For a few moments they sat in silence, listening to the conversation around them, which was mostly in French and Chinese.

Baine turned to the *maître d'* who had come up behind him with the news that their meal had now been prepared and awaited them as soon as they were settled at their table, which he hoped they would like.

They were shown to the table and Blaine expressed approval. Soon afterwards their food arrived, and for a time they were too occupied with eating it to talk.

Finally, the strained meal—which ended with tiny Island strawberries in Cointreau—was over, and Syrie reached for her peach-coloured bag and they walked back to where Blaine's car was parked. She did not bother to remind him that they had intended to visit some of the shops with the exciting names.

As they left Curepipe behind, her eyes brooded on the sugar cane which, she knew, grew almost down to the beaches. The road seemed to be littered with sticks of cane, which must have dropped off every single truck carrying them from the fields to the mills.

'Thank you,' she said, 'for the lunch, Blaine. The food was excellent.'

'I'm glad you enjoyed it.' His voice was hard.

To break another long silence she said, 'The architecture was very French, of course. I was surprised to see the enormous fireplace which, I suppose, is hardly ever used.'

'Well, as usual, you suppose wrong. It *is* used. It's often cold in Curepipe at night. Being so high up, it is often beneath cloud and drizzle. Syrie, this absurd and one-sided conversation has gone on long enough. Let's face it, you're not thinking about Curepipe and huge fireplaces right now, and neither am I.'

She turned to look at him. 'Don't be angry, Blaine. I

realise I spoilt lunch by bringing Craig's name up, and I'm sorry, honestly, but you must admit this is the most bizarre thing. Sometimes I can hardly believe it's all happening—that he's gone and I don't know what's going to happen.'

'What *should* happen is that you should forget him. Tell me, what did you have in mind when you came to marry him? Being his devoted handmaiden? Preparing his food? Massaging his poor, aching back after a long, hard day at the studio, where he was *so overworked* that he couldn't find the time to remember the date of your arrival?' Blaine had reverted to cutting sarcasm.

Oh, I'm going to howl, she found herself thinking. Please don't let me. Taking her bottom lip between her teeth, she reached for her bag and searched for a tissue.

'It's a bit late in the day for tears, Syrie.' There was cruel mockery behind the words.

Dabbing at her eyes she said, 'Stop acting like a pig!'

He laughed softly. 'I am a pig, but at least I'm an honest pig.'

'Don't mock me, Blaine. I'm upset enough as it is. Can't you see that?'

'I *can* see that. What I can't see, though, is *why*? Why go on torturing yourself over this son of a bitch?'

Syrie tensed as he slowed down and pulled into the side of the road and then into one of the private roads which always went in straight lines through the fields.

By this time she had pulled herself together and was using a fresh tissue and a mirror to repair the damage to her face which had been caused by tears.

Blaine positioned himself so that he could place his hands on her shoulders. Not very gently, he turned her round so that she was looking at him.

'So—you're without the man you love and believe in?'

'Yes, I am, but it's not the end of the damned world

for me.'

'That's what I'm trying to tell you.' His fingers were beneath her hair now.

'Just take your fingers out of my hair, if you don't mind. I don't need this sort of attention from you, Blaine.'

He held her gaze. 'No? We'll see about that.' He bent his head to kiss her and, typically of him, he demanded a response from her lips. Syrie found herself wanting to cling to him and to pretend that Craig had never happened.

Blaine shattered her by saying, 'Shall we go back to your hotel and pursue this? Between us, Syrie, lies the chemistry to blow all the extinct volcano craters on the island to smithereens. I want to undress you, do you know that? I want to make love to you, but I'm certainly not going to do it here.'

She pushed him away. 'You've got a hope!'

'That's your opinion. I happen not to agree.' He started the car.

Syrie sat back, angry and humiliated at the longing he had aroused in her which would not go away.

He turned to look at her. 'What are we going to do about this? Are we going to have an affair until you work things out with your fiancée? I wasn't blind to your arousal just now.'

His quickness in wanting to make love to her—and her to him—had unnerved her.

'This conversation strikes me as quite callous. How am I going to work for Design Dimension if this is the sort of behaviour I can expect from you, Blaine? Let's get this one thing straight. I feel nothing for you.'

'In that case, maybe I just caught you in one of your eager-for-sexual-gratification moments?' He strung the words along. 'Huh, Syrie?'

'Why don't you add—from Athens, and be done with it? You seem to get *such* a kick out of calling me Syrie from Athens. That remark, to me, is a classic example of discrimination. What's so unusual about that? Or, chauvinistic pig that you are, do you believe that being eager for sexual gratification is something only the male of the species is entitled to? Having you, or any other man, for that matter, make love to me at this present time is the last thing on my mind. And, by the way, it might just interest you to know that nothing happened in Athens. In other words, I did *not* go to bed with Craig in Athens. For one thing, I have never wanted to feel manipulated into a situation.'

'In other words, you never really trusted him. You didn't trust him then—if you're honest with yourself—and you don't trust him now. It irritates me that you're so inconsistent.'

'I don't want to talk to you. Just get me to your house where I can get into Craig's car and drive to my hotel.'

Later, he waited while she got into the car, which she had left parked in the driveway. Before she drove off, he turned and made his way towards the steps leading to the veranda.

He phoned her the following morning, early.

'Syrie?'

'Yes?' Her voice was brittle.

'There's a letter waiting for you. Craig's handwriting appears on the envelope and it was posted in Réunion.' He laughed nastily. 'Maybe this guy is cut out to make a fabulous husband, after all? Well, you were a fabulous catch, let's face it. He won't be all that anxious to lose you. You must have been like a godsend to him, Syrie.'

She remained very calm. 'Stop pressuring me. I'll be over for my letter. I'm not quite sure when, though.'

'You'd better make it soon. You see, there's something

else . . .'

She realised how tense she was. 'And—that is?'

'It concerns Craig's car.'

'Suppose you get to the point? I'm busy right now.' She took a breath.

'It has been discovered that Craig had been double discounting, and that he raised two loans from different sources in order to buy the same vehicle. He has not repaid the sum owed to either.'

She felt a rush of adrenalin. 'What does that mean?'

'It means, quite simply, that the car will be reclaimed. In other words, you will have to hand it over and you will now be without a car. Another thing, I had to sign for a letter of demand, addressed to you personally. By that, I mean it was not addressed to Craig. It comes from . . . let me see—the name is on the back of the envelope.'

'I *know* the name! You don't have to bother to strain those poor eyes of yours. I notice that at times you wear *big* glasses, or is that just for—effect?'

The demand, she was thinking, would be for goods which Craig must have purchased—no doubt to barter with. On receipt of the first account, she had felt shocked at the amount, and yet Craig had had nothing to show for his shopping spree. What was more, he had not mentioned the fact that he had been buying. When it came to settling one of his countless debts, he must have come to an arrangement where he would offer *goods*, instead of cash.

After this news, passed on to her by Blaine, she felt half-wild with rage. What had Craig done to her? His letter could wait and so could the car, unless someone came to the hotel for it.

For the first time in her life, she thought, Syrie Knight—*from Athens*—felt like going out somewhere and getting blind drunk. She had believed herself to be so in love with Craig that, when he'd asked her to marry him she had thrown all caution to the winds and accepted his proposal.

Still, the sweet memories came rushing in. Memories of sightseeing together, including Delphi. She had been so in love that she'd asked for unpaid leave from her firm so that she and Craig could spend long, wonderful days together. She thought about the day in Athens when she'd introduced him to Turkish coffee, and how she had laughed at his face as he'd drunk it.

Shoving the momories to one side, she allowed her fury to break, and in the privacy of her hotel room she began to throw things about: soft things—like her clothing and her slippers. She kicked out at things and then turned her attention to the wicker dressing-table. It was nothing short of a brainstorm and then she collapsed, in pain, on her bed. I've broken my toe, she thought, wanting to faint. Although on inspection her toe appeared to be intact, she began to howl. She had been reduced to nothing. Nothing! She found herself wishing she was a sailor—drunk and in port—and she had visions of smashed chairs and overturned tables.

The next morning, her toe was black and blue and very swollen. She could not wear a shoe and looked out the plastic slip-ons which she had bought to protect her feet from the coral which often littered the beaches.

Thank goodness, she thought, I'm not married to him.

At the end of the week she scooped her cosmetics and perfume flagons from the dressing-table and slipped them into her overnight bag. She grabbed her toothbrush and toothpaste from the bathroom, along with one or two other items, and put them into a plastic-lined floral bag. Finally, she slid back the wardrobe doors and took out the clothes she'd brought with her to the hotel. Whatever it was—was over.

After settling her account, she got into Craig's car, which would no longer be at her disposal. Well, she'd purchase her own car, she thought angrily. No problem, as they always said in Mauritius. A small, economic-to-run, efficient car.

By the time she parked the car in the driveway of Blaine's stately old mansion, there was nothing to show the terrible stress she had endured at the hotel; she looked casually elegant in a black and white spotted cotton sateen jacket and black trousers. Black beads hung over the white shirt to go with the outfit. When she had chosen clothes for her trousseau, she had only chosen items which really excited her.

She went upstairs to the room which held such conflicting memories for her. Liselle had arranged roses in a dusky-pink bowl, and Craig's letter was propped against it.

Crossing over to the table, she picked up the envelope and eased it open with one long oval fingernail.

There was no address in Réunion. Well, that figures, she thought bitterly.

'Syrie, my darling,' she read, 'by the time you get this, Réunion and Mauritius will both be in the past, for me, and my heart aches. For obvious reasons, I can't possibly give you an address. I am giving this letter to someone who will post it after my plane has left here. Since I know this person'—would it be Hélène? Syrie wondered—'I am sure you will receive it.

'You've got to believe this, Sy.'—Sy this and Sy that—as Blaine would have said, she thought—'I have been framed. In Australia'—Syrie's heart froze, for, although her feelings for Craig had taken a smashing, she did not want him caught and sent to jail—'I got into debt and was helped by a man who specialised in that sort of thing with considerable success, I might add, since he nearly always terminated such dealings in blackmailing his client. I was one of them. I couldn't bring myself to tell you about that part of my life. I came to Mauritius and tried to start a new life. I got to know Blaine, who eventually offered me a partnership in Design Demension. He didn't know it, of course, but I had to borrow most of the money—well—all of it, really. I had other debts and so I borrowed quite a lot of money. In the end, I was being harrassed from every quarter—this moneylender and so on and so on. The old nightmare, for me, had started all over again. Lately, threats from this man in Port Louis have become dangerously real. On what was supposed to have been our wedding day, he sent one of his tough stooges to terrorise me. Soon afterwards I had no option but to clear out—leaving you. You'll never know what that did to me, Sy. I cannot say, at this stage, what my plans are, but as soon as I can I'll send for you.'

Well, let's face it, she thought, as Blaine's cruel words came to mind, I was a fabulous catch, Craig. You won't want to lose out, will you?

Her eyes went on skimming the words. They almost 'whined' at her from their positions on the notepaper. Craig tried to explain how he had 'borrowed' money from Design Dimension and how he had intended to pay it back.

'Blaine,' Craig ended, 'will say I've swindled him, which is nonsense . . . I just got out of my depth.'

'Oh, Craig . . .' Syrie said aloud. Feeling nothing but depression, she folded the letter and put it away, and then she went downstairs to the studio.

CHAPTER EIGHT

DIRECTLY Blaine saw her he said, 'So, Syrie? What's the pronounced limp in aid of?'

'Very possibly I have a fractured toe.' Her voice was cool.

'How did that happen?' She was aware of his interest.

She lifted her elegant shoulders, and in a theatrical voice answered, 'Oh, it was self-inflicted. I kicked it.'

She saw the mockery in his blue eyes. 'Where did this self-inflicted injury take place?'

'It took place at the hotel, and if you are waiting for more details, which I suspect you are, against the wicker dressing-table.'

'In other words, when you became aware of the fact that you've been taken for a ride!'

'In other words, for a few minutes I had violent symptoms of mental disturbance—*yes*. However, I am back to normal. You're so sweet, Blaine, to have noticed my limp. There's not much I can get away with, is there?' Her voice was bitter.

'It's just my way of saying—I told you so.'

'Of course. I realise that.' She stared at him angrily. 'Blaine, as you can see, I'm limping—but I'm back. Now, I know I'm not supposed to start work until Monday, but is there anything you would like me to do *now*?'

Ignoring her question he said, 'What did he say in his letter?'

'He said—*in many ways*—he'd been framed.'

Blaine's laugh was soft. 'Framed? And you believe him?'

After a slight hesitation she said, 'Yes, in some instances—I guess he was framed.'

'In—some instances, who is supposed to have framed him, pray?' The hard streak in Blaine was to the fore.

'Somebody in Australia and also Jubala Jurrah, I should imagine.'

'Framed? Don't make me laugh, Syrie. They all come up with the same old pathetic story—I was framed! The same old whine. Where has he gone? Did he say where he was going? I'm sure he must have left Réunion by now. Since he has become quite an expert on fleeing from one country to another, he probably lost no time in raising more money somewhere. I'd be interest to examine Craig's brainbox, actually.'

'I'm sure you would. You'd love to take it to pieces—grain by grain, wouldn't you? You're very callous, Blaine.'

'There are times when I *have* to be. And—does he intend sending for you when he reaches Shangri-La?' Blaine's blue eyes were hard. 'His new Shangri-La.'

'He intends sending for me, yes.'

'Hah! And you will go straight to him, of course. Let's just hope you're not too old to make the journey. That would really floor him. To lose out on what might still be left of that inheritance . . . tut, tut.' He swung himself on his swivel chair and looked up at her.

Syrie stared back at him. 'Well, do I start trying to make myself useful here or not? If so, what do you want me to do?'

'Well, let's see.' He glanced round at the activity in the studio. 'In a few moments we are about to do a shoot. Nothing special. Maybe you should start by watching.'

'I'd like that,' she answered, eager to get off the subject of Craig; before she remembered the car. 'By the way, the car is parked outside. What shall I do about it?'

'Leave everything to me. I'll arrange for it to be picked up.' Blaine got up from his desk and went to another part of the studio, and when he came back he said, 'Sit over there—out of the way.' Her eyes went to the wicker peacock chair which stood against the long wall of small-paned windows, and then she went over to the chair and sat down.

When Blaine joined her he said, 'Let me explain. This is to be an advert for shirts. Not very exciting, but it will give you an insight into what goes on around here from time to time. Mostly we do our photography elsewhere, but in a case like this the studio is adequate. OK?' He gave her one of his irresistible smiles.

She did not smile back. 'Yes.'

Andy Midrand and Les Lauder were busy pinning a shirt into place so that it would not sag in the wrong places. The model looked like the sexy hunk of Mauritius.

'Ah, that's a nice clinging line,' Andy was saying. 'I'll tell you something, though, Giraud—this is going to make you feel like giving up modelling for life. I don't want you to move—not even an eyelash—once I've got you behind this desk. Here's the folder. Hold it. *That's* it. You're a high-powered executive, right? Yes, I like that relaxed look, but don't move. Now, let's see how it looks from behind here.' He went towards one of the cameras on tripods. 'Move that hazy light over there. It's in the wrong place, and another thing, I don't like the position of that plant. Hey, we can't use that picture on the wall behind the desk.'

Les looked impatient. 'Why not, Andy?'

'It's too shiny. Look, Les, take the glass out of the frame. That'll solve the problem.'

'That's impossible, Andy. I borrowed this picture from Tony. It's one of his prized possessions, actually. He'll kill me if it gets damaged.'

Beside her, Syrie heard Blaine laugh. It was a nice laugh and she looked round at him. He was half sitting on an L-shaped desk. 'Andy, if that picture is damaged, I can tell you now, Les will lose his lifelong friend.'

'Yeah,' Les added, 'and there goes my listening to music in Tony's flat. Look, let's spray the glass. That will solve everything. Do you have a can of deodorant, Blaine?'

Blaine laughed again. 'It might not work, but we'll have a go, anyway.' He turned to looked at Syrie. 'Would you mind going upstairs? There should be something in my room—or my bathroom.'

'This is a big house.' Her voice was like ice. 'How should I know where your room is?' Damn you, she thought, what are you trying to get across to everyone? That you've already staked your claim?

His smile was devilish. 'It's down the passage from yours. You can't miss it.'

Trying not to show how ruffled she was, she stood up and made her way towards the hall.

Blaine's room had a distinctly oriental flavour, but this was probably because Curepipe and Port Louis shops had much to offer. The bed, she noticed, was kingsize with a red-lacquered cane head-rest. The low bedside tables, upon which stood brass-based lamps, were also made of cane, lacquered red. A navy bedspread, red-checked and flared, added drama, and the room was fitted with a pale blue carpet. Looking at it, Syrie found herself wondering whether Hélène had lain by Blaine's side in this room, after the nice old-fashioned housekeeper had retired for the night.

She went into the adjoining bathroom and chose a spray which she took along to the studio.

Les immediately began to protest about spraying the glass.

'What if it gets behind the glass?' he asked.

Syrie was longing to suggest that they use another picture. After all, Blaine's house was filled with pictures, and there was bound to be one which would look as good behind the desk and to one side of the plant, which had been arranged to resemble a corner of an office, but since she was only starting work on Monday she thought best to keep quiet.

Andy was beginning to sound irritated now.

'What's all the fuss about? The frame is sealed. Besides, if the worst comes to the worst we can have the picture taken out and the glass cleaned and re-sealed with brown paper.'

'Another thing,' Les argued, 'you're going to stuff up the wall with that spray.'

Syrie had to keep herself from laughing outright.

By this time the studio was filled with spray and Giraud, the model, held his nose. 'I wish to sneeze,' he called out. 'What about the pins in the shirt? Will they hold?'

'Don't sneeze,' Andy shouted. 'If you do, Giraud, you'll bugger the shirt up.'

Andy was instantly aware of Syrie's presence the moment he had sworn.

'Sorry about that, Syrie. I'm afraid nobody cared

much when Peta was here.'

Blaine came to stand next to her, and she was more than just a little aware of his white cotton-clad thighs. He bent his head and said lightly, 'Come along, Syrie. I have a feeling that if I stay here I'm going to fire someone.'

Feeling totally carefree at this moment, she laughed up at him. 'Not me, I hope? Before I've even started work?'

For a moment, the space between them seemed charged. 'OK?' He held out a hand and she found herself taking it as he helped her from the chair.

When they were in the hall he said, 'I have an appointment in Port Louis after lunch. It will last until well after five, and since I worked until well after midnight, I guess I need a break. Let's go to the beach.'

'I have things to do,' she hedged. 'Since I'm not needed in the studio I'll . . .'

He cut in. 'Come on. You don't expect me to fall for that one, do you? Anyway, what kind of things?'

She lifted her shoulders. 'Well . . . I'm expecting my things to arrive from Athens any day now.'

'Does that mean today?' His eyes mocked her.

She laughed. 'Not today, maybe, but—one can never be sure, after all.'

'Be ready in ten minutes.' He left her and took the stairs two at a time, and after a moment she followed him.

Later, and wearing a black one-piece swimsuit, cut to flatter and patterned with big pink and yellow hibiscus flowers and green leaves, she sat next to Blaine on the sun-drenched beach. Her matching big 'show-off' shirt lay next to her, where she had carelessly tossed it.

Blaine went to sit at her feet. 'Let me see your foot, which you have so artfully buried in the sand.' He grinned boyishly and, before she could stop him, he made a grab for her ankle.

'Don't you dare!' She pushed her foot deeper into the fine sand.

Since he was not wearing a shirt and because of his tan, Blaine's eyes appeared more blue than ever. Syrie's eyes went to the pull-on shorts he was wearing, which were the same colour as the yellow blooms on her swimsuit and big shirt.

Without warning, he grabbed her ankle and lifted her foot, and she felt something like a bolt of lightning pass right through her.

'It's very bruised,' he said softly. He lifted his dark lashes. 'What were you trying to do? Break it?'

'Yes. I was.' She tried again to free her foot from his grasp, but he held on to it and then he began to massage it carefully.

'The whole foot is bruised. You must have been pretty mad to kick out like that.'

'I told you—I showed violent symptoms of mental disturbance. In other words, I had a brainstorm.'

Both were aware of a strong physical attraction. She watched him as he lifted her foot and begin to kiss it, keeping his eyes on her face.

'You look beautiful,' he told her. 'Whatever you happen to be wearing—you look wonderful.'

When she answered, her tone was almost artificial. 'Well, after all, I love clothes. Perhaps I spend too much on them. Strangely enough, all the positions I held necessitated grooming on my part—especially the one I had in Athens.'

She could have kicked herself for mentioning Athens.

Blaine rested her foot on his sun-warmed thigh and began to massage it.

'Are we going to become lovers, Syrie?' He held her eyes with his own, and she felt a distinct element of fear, because she now wanted it so much.

After a moment she said, 'I'm not on the market as a stand-in for Hélène—and just because Craig happens to be away.' In one fluid movement, she pulled her foot away and stood up. 'I thought we came to swim?'

'We're going to swim,' he answered.

'Well, I'm going in now.'

When the water was up to her thighs, she did a neat dive and began to swim underwater. When she surfaced, he was at her side and so she swam away from him, kicking her feet to create plenty of spray.

After a while, she turned over and began to float on her back.

'What are you thinking about?' Blaine asked, beside her.

She stood up. The water reached her bosom and she moved her hands beneath the water.

'I was thinking—I had such great expectations, you know. I just don't believe all this.'

'Don't you *want* to believe it?' When she did not answer he said, 'This attitude you've adopted about Craig strikes me as totally dishonest. Actually, it's a joke.'

'Why dishonest, Blaine? And what's so funny about being jilted—to use that nice old-fashioned word? You might try being a little more sympathetic towards me, if nothing else.'

'You want it both ways, don't you?' His eyes were blazing.

'What do you mean—I want it both ways?'

'You want me and you want him, or so you'd have

me believe.' He caught her by the shoulders. 'But you are now in a position where you want to play the temptress.'

She twisted herself free of him and began to wade through the water towards the beach. Soon afterwards he followed her.

She was towelling her legs and she did not look up, and then, taking four wooden bangles from the pocket of her shirt, she slipped them on to her wrist where they immediately began to rattle about as she moved.

When she straightened, their eyes met and something ignited between them. Suddenly and urgently, he caught her to him and she drew a quick breath as she felt his near-naked body next to her own. He put his fingers beneath her chin and tilted her face so that he could kiss her. She kissed him back and felt thrilled to the soles of her feet.

When his hand went to her breast, she came to her senses.

'No. Don't do that. That's—not—what I want.'

'Do you know what the hell you want?' He was instantly angry. 'You keep ignoring the signs, Syrie. If Craig has been married before—and, subconsciously, I've been thinking about this—he must have let *her* down. He's let *you* down. Right? For what it's worth—he's let me down. He's let that rat Jurrah down—and goodness knows how many other people. But he still can't see that he's let you down because he is determined to get you. You're worth hanging on to.'

'Don't say these things. You love seeing me in a state of high-grade stress, don't you?' She shoved her hands through her tawny hair. 'You won't be satisfied until you have my back to the wall. Is this what you did to Craig, I wonder?'

'Whatever has happened to Craig, he's done to

himself.'

'I don't believe he's been responsible for—*everything* that's gone wrong in his life.' Stooping, she reached for her hibiscus-patterned shirt and shrugged herself into it.

'Because you don't *want* to believe it! Your stubborn pride won't let you believe it. OK, Syrie . . .'

'Syrie from Athens!' she cut in, almost shouting the words at him. 'Don't forget my name tag.'

On the day she started work, it was Andy Midrand who showed her around Design Dimension. He went to considerable length explaining what the job deadline board was all about; where the slide files were kept; what light-boxes were used for and why they used hazy lights.

In the weeks that followed Blaine mentioned that she was to canvass for Design Dimension—in other words, she would be expected to work on bringing in new accounts; accounts which would grow. For this work she would need a car and since Craig's car had now been reclaimed she was to use a Mini which belonged to the business.

For another two weeks she watched the entire staff at work, helping wherever she could, and she was also shown the latest audio-visual presentation, which was screened to potential clients to promote the studio's expertise in advertising.

Blaine had shown her the audio-visual one night.

That very day, Syrie had received a letter and certain documents advising her that her belongings had arrived from Athens, and she asked for time off to drive to Port Louis to arrange the necessary transport from the docks to Blaine's house, where a number of items would go into a store-room and others into the room which she was using.

In her ignorance of such matters, and not wanting to

consult Blaine about it, she had gone from one tiny office to another with the papers in her possession. She caused raised eyebrows when, quite by accident, she found herself in the dry-dock area.

Some of the warehouses lining the waterfront, she was told by a willing guide who had decided to help her, dated from the French East Company days.

Somebody else, who also tried to be of assistance to her, pointed out Spear Grass Peak and explained that morning cloud obscured the other peaks of the Moka range.

It was an efficient small port. She could see that, but she had become lost and confused. Eventually, the nightmare was over and, hot and bothered, she arrived back to discover a message to the effect that a number of items, belonging to Craig and stored in the outbuildings of the small shop owned by a Creole couple, were to be reclaimed, since they had not been paid for. This was further proof of Craig's web of doubt.

By the time Blaine suggested the screening of the audio-visual, she was more than ready to fall into bed.

He had been cool to her since the day they had gone to the beach together.

'Come on, Syrie.' He sounded annoyed. 'Isn't it about time you paid attention? You look so "switched off". You might as well know it; you will have to show this presentation yourself in the very near future. This is what it's all about—to show potential clients what they can expect from us.'

'I'm not switched off. I'm tired, though. I had an awful time in Port Louis today. As you already know, I had to ask for more time off to sort something out with regard to Craig's belongings . . .' Blaine interrupted rudely. 'I don't need a post-mortem on Craig's belongings. Let's just get on with the matter on hand.'

She felt like pointing out that it was, in fact, after

hours, but she kept quiet.

Blaine began to pour wine, which he had brought along to the studio, and then he passed her a chilled glass.

'OK,' he said a moment later, 'let's get this rolling, shall we?'

There was always this ruthless streak in him, she thought resentfully. *He* was full of energy and it was a case of—I'm all right, Jack, pull up the ladder.

As though he could read her thoughts, he glanced at her and their eyes clashed. 'It's no use glaring at me like that,' he said. 'It's not my fault you've decided to work out Craig's problems while he's on the run.'

She did not answer, and while he set things up she sat back and sipped her wine and let her gaze wander around the empty studio. It was all so familiar now, she thought—a part of her life—the white-tiled floor and oriental rugs, white L-shaped desks, slide projectors, stereo amplifiers, electronic flash units and tripods . . . even the dogs, Raizel and Rascal played their role.

Raizel was in her basket near the french doors, and it was obvious that she was dreaming. After watching the twitching and listening to the whimpering noises for a while, Syrie put down her glass and went to pat the beagle.

'Stop fidgeting, Syrie.' Blaine made no attempt to disguise the fact that she was irritating him. 'You're beginning to get on my damned nerves.'

'I was only trying to soothe her. She's having a nightmare!' Syrie sat back on her heels and looked across at him. Her dress had crept up over her tanned thighs, and Blaine's eyes flickered over them.

'I don't care if she's having a nightmare. Dogs are always dreaming.'

She took a ragged breath. 'Well, I do care, Blaine. I'm

not as callous as you are.'

'There's nothing callous about it. Raizel sleeps here every night, and she copes quite well with her nightmares. So what are you meddling for? It doesn't make sense, but then, a lot of what you do doesn't make sense to *me*.'

Stung by his sarcasm, she stood up and gave him an angry look, then went back to her wine and sat down.

Even though she was so exhausted, the presentation gripped her, and at the end of it she said, 'It's very good, Blaine.'

'And so you were interested?'

'Yes. Very interested.'

'Is that why you've looked at your watch at least fifty times?' he asked sarcastically.

'That's just not true, and you know it!'

He came over to her and took her glass. 'Let me pour you some wine.'

The studio was almost in darkness now, except for one small lamp which he had turned on.

'Thank you. I might as well add a hangover to my list of miseries.'

'What are you miserable about now?'

'Well, for one thing, I have a headache. Perhaps I should say—I *already* have a headache. For another, I'm worried.'

'You're worried, huh? Well, that's nothing new. After all, this guy's given you enough to keep you worried for the rest of your life, if you're stupid enough to accept this state of affairs.' He sighed loudly and his sarcastic, uncaring attitude rattled her. 'If you want to go on feeling duty-bound, what do you expect?'

'And—what do *you* expect, Blaine? Do you think I can just sweep my obligations beneath a rug?'

'*What* obligations?' He sounded frankly angry.

'There are matters which concern me, such as debts incurred as a result of the reception. These debts didn't just revolve around Craig. Craig did the organising and, since he seemed to have accounts all over the place, I didn't argue. I mean,' she lifted her hands, 'we—ah—fully intended to pay . . .'

'Don't make me break down laughing, Syrie.'

'As it happens, I will settle all these accounts myself, directly they come to hand. Another thing, I'd be a fine one if I didn't try to sort out his belongings, wouldn't I? There's nobody here, it would seem, to see to these matters. You certainly aren't going to interest yourself.'

Since she was sitting and he was standing, she tilted her head back to look at him. He caught her gaze and held it, and the atmosphere between them became tense.

'I notice you're not wearing your ring.'

'For the simple reason that I took it off,' she retorted.

'For cleaning purposes—or are you no longer engaged to him?'

'I think that's my affair, Blaine. I don't have to explain everything.'

'You've been making a jolly good attempt, haven't you? You have one topic of conversation—Craig.'

She stood up. 'Please don't lock the door. I'm going out—but I will be back shortly.'

'Where are you going?' he asked.

'Just for a *walk*, Blaine.' She felt irritable beyond words. 'This headache is wearing me down.'

'You can add my headache to the list.' He went to turn off the lamp. 'I'll come with you.'

They were in the garden when she said, 'You know you always speak about Craig as one would discuss a criminal. Nevertheless, you saw fit to have him as a partner—or have you forgotten so quickly?'

'I haven't forgotten. He left me all the reason in the

world to remember. Let's say, he left a nice hole in my bank balance, as it were—and he left me *you*.' Blaine's voice was hard.

'Would you like me to go?' she asked, feeling something like an ice-cold rubber band around her heart.

'When I want you to go, I'll tell you,' he told her shortly.

'To get back to the accounts . . .'

'Must we get back to them?' he asked angrily.

Sick with humiliation, she said, '*Yes*. We must. When I made enquiries, I was told that you have paid some of them—the reception accounts, I mean. Can you tell my why, Blaine?'

He did not respond to her question.

'Blaine?' In the darkness, she saw him wave off the remark.

'Forget about it.'

After a long moment she said in a stifled voice, 'You've paid, haven't you? Without my knowledge. Well!' she released a breath. 'What else—in my life?'

He took her hand. 'Let's sit on the sand. It's time we began to relax.'

'I really don't want to sit down.'

'Must you always argue?' he asked. He virtually pulled her down beside him. 'Now, relax!'

'Relax?' she asked, angrily. 'I wish you hadn't done that. Do you know how bad this makes me feel? I want to *see* the accounts you've paid. They concern the catering of what was supposed to have been my wedding reception. How did they get into your hands in the first place?'

'You've got enough on your mind, as it is. You can pay me back later.' He drew her close and she rested her aching head on his shoulder. That was what

Craig kept saying to me, she thought bitterly—I'll pay you back later, Sy.

In a few moments she said, 'You know, Blaine, after my parents died I found myself in control of a very adequate income. I'm referring to my inheritance, of course. In other words, I was left considerably well-off, but I have always been very careful. As you know, wherever I have travelled, I have worked in that particular country. I worked in Holland, Paris . . .'

He cut in and she immediately realised that he was trying to get her off the subject of Craig, which was bound to crop up.

'What kind of work did you do in Paris?'

'I was a buyer for a boutique named Chez Michi. Actually, I was very happy there, but to get back to my inheritance . . . I only realise now that I made the biggest mistake of my life when I told Craig about my affairs, but I trusted him.'

She was silent for a long time, and then she went on, while Blaine stroked her hair.

'I thought I'd found my mate—you know. We seemed to have so much in common. Craig seemed to add up to everything I thought I wanted in a man. For one thing, he was always so gentle, and I needed that, believe me.'

'Well, let's face it,' Blaine answered, 'Craig's got a lot going for him, after all. In this case, it paid him to be gentle with you. He knew you'd suffered. Behind those gentle ways of his, there's a hard, calculating streak. Even I have found that out.'

Blaine moved his position so that he could gather her into his arms. He held her close and his lips brushed her forehead, her temples and then went to her lips. He was interested only in making love to her. She knew that.

Against his mouth she murmured, 'For the second time in my life, I feel fractured. That's the only way I can describe it.'

'Don't let's talk about Craig now. We've got to start thinking about us. We've wasted too much time as it is.' There was tension in Blaine's voice. 'I want you so much. I want to make love to you.' She could feel his need of her and it frightened her.

'Blaine, no!' She pushed him away. 'I don't want to find myself in deep waters with you. I've had enough of all that, believe me.'

He was silent for several minutes and she could hear his breathing. Finally, he stood up and reached for her hand and pulled her up beside him.

'OK, Syrie, let's go. After all, *buying* your services— by employing you at Design Dimension—did not enter into the agreement. Go ahead and save yourself for this gentle guy with his Sy this and Sy that, if that's want you want.'

As they walked back to the house, she made a big show of brushing the sand from her legs, arms and dress, but she was trying to hide the fact that she was crying.

By the time they reached the steps up to the veranda she had recovered. 'I'm not ready for anything to happen between us.'

'But you *want* it to happen when you're ready, whenever that will be. That's right, isn't it?' His voice was hard. 'You appear to be finding it difficult to make up your mind about Craig. Anyway, what is more important to me right now is a nightcap. Maybe you'd like to join me? I'm going along to the study.'

Syrie found that she was hurt at his tone, but tried not to show it.

'I'd love some orange juice. Nothing stronger. I'm

afraid the sea air did nothing for my headache. I'll go
up to my room first for a couple of pain-killers.'

'Fine,' he answered curtly.

She left him and then went up to her room for the
pills, and a few minutes later joined Blaine in the
study, where he passed her a glass of juice which he
had taken from the small bar refrigerator.

'I'm feeling very upset,' she said, giving him a long
look. 'You might as well know it.'

'Well, Syrie, I thought you'd given up dedicating
your life to Craig, but it looks as if I was wrong.' He
lifted his glass. 'I salute you. Your concern is very
touching.'

'I'm upset about the accounts and I'm upset about
his belongings. I came here to marry him . . .'

'And he walked out on you . . .' Blaine cut in
brutally.

'He had no option. It would appear that there is just
no one in Mauritius to sort things out for him—once
I've decided what to do about his . . .'

'I'm not interested! One thing, though—you know
we both wanted what could have happened tonight,
the first time we met. Now that he's gone—what
stands in the way?'

'Blaine, I believed I had made the right choice when
I came to Mauritius to marry Craig, and I was not
going to allow the fact that you excited me to get in
the way. I felt something for you at the airport that
day, I'll be honest and—I—still feel something, but—
I'm not ready to leap into another relationship.'

'Forget about the relationship!' His face was ex-
pressionless as he turned off the reading lamp and
opened the door. 'After you.'

She gazed at him for a moment. 'How I live is my
own concern. If I choose to help Craig by seeing what

belongs to him and what doesn't it has very little to do with you.' She lifted her hands. 'I mean—everybody seems to be stepping in and reclaiming this and reclaiming that. Surely Craig must legally possess *some* things? OK, so he might have left me on our wedding day . . .'

'He left you to face the music, you silly little fool. When are you going to face up to that?'

'I *have* faced up to it, but anyone can see that he is a very desperate man, Blaine.' Why was she going on like this? she asked herself. Was it to show Blaine that she was not looking for a 'new romance'? To prove to him that she was just not that kind of girl? Or was it because, deep down, there was still something left for Craig? In the thick of her 'brainstorm' she had pulled her engagement ring from her finger and hidden it away in a drawer.

'Let's drop this. I've had enough of Craig Knox for one night. Are you ready, Syrie? I'm waiting—or do you want to spend the night here in the study?'

'Why are you always so cruel?' she asked.

'What would you like to hear me say? That if I *am* cruel, it is the cruelty of jealousy?'

He left her, to check that the big doors leading from the hall to the veranda were locked, and she took this opportunity of going upstairs by herself.

There were gold-wrapped chocolates on her pillows, and the bedcovers had been turned back. This was Liselle's special routine, and Syrie stared at the chocolates before she picked them up and put them into a drawer. She had made a mistake in confiding in Blaine. Under no conceivable circumstance would she ever permit her life to go out of control again, she told herself angrily.

CHAPTER NINE

DAYS turned into weeks, and Syrie worked on being calm and in control of her life. She also concentrated on her work, which she found interesting.

Due to an upset in their original plans, the people who were in the chalet which she and Craig had agreed to rent asked for permission to stay on. In a weak moment she had agreed to this, and as a result was still staying in Blaine's house.

She had not seen her way clear enough to buy a car at the moment, and was using the car belonging to Design Dimension, since her work entailed a certain amount of travelling about. Fortunately, she thought, she had an international driver's licence.

On several occasions Blaine paid her compliments, but these compliments merely revolved around her work.

'I'm glad you thought of this,' he said one afternoon, referring to the fact that she always made a point of sending a prospective client a letter, summarising the reasons why Design Dimension should be the obvious choice when it came to advertising.

As he bent over her desk, she felt her nerves begin to tighten. Clearing her throat, she passed him the name and address of a new cosmetic company.

'I really thought I was on to something good here, but I'm investigating a credit risk. I'm not too happy about these people. They seem to be functioning on a shoestring.'

'Oh, well, I know you'll use your initiative, Syrie—in business, if not in a *personal capacity*.' He turned to look at her and she saw the hard mockery in his eyes.

Sheer anger prevented her from answering.

In the background, Andy was talking to one of the commercial artists who had come through.

'I think this is too eccentric, Shulah. Why not keep the illustrations simple?'

If only I could keep *my life simple*, Syrie found herself thinking, feeling frustrated and restless all of a sudden. How have I changed so much since meeting up with Craig?

Blaine always seemed to pick up her thoughts.

'I take it you have still not heard from your fiancé?' His tone was baiting.

'Believe me, Blaine, you would have been the first to know. After all, you are also involved, one way and another. Right?' Her green eyes looked back at him coolly.

He smiled suddenly. 'I was just asking. Anyway, I think this latest contract you've managed to rope in calls for a celebratory dinner. How about tonight?'

Why not? she thought. 'That sounds nice. Where?'

'Pack an overnight bag, and you'll see. This is strictly on the level, by the way. The place I want to take you to involves an overnight stop. If we leave in about an hour's time, we'll reach there by sunset. That's taking it slowly, so that you can take in a bit of the countryside.'

She didn't argue. Suddenly, she didn't want to argue. She just wanted to be with him.

'It sounds interesting. I'll look forward to it.'

Good. In that case, let's call it a day here.'

He took her to a place called Trou aux Biches which, he explained, meant Crater of the Does. This was because there was a small water-hole which had been a crater, at one time, in an area where the Java deer came to drink.

As Blaine had intimated, they had taken their time getting here, and it was practically dark by the time he parked the car.

Immediately upon contacting the desk personnel at reception, they were informed that it was just as well they had booked in advance, for the exotic village hotel complex was fully booked and ready for fun—naturally. They were given an invitation to a cocktail party which was to be held at a nearby chalet which seemed to be reserved for this purpose.

'To welcome you,' it was explained, smilingly.

The chalets which made up the 'village' were all A-framed—two chalets downstairs and one running the full length of the building upstairs. Blaine was booked in downstairs, and Syrie's accommodation was in the chalet above.

They waited while the porter unlocked the coral door and carried Blaine's overnight bag into his chalet and then they went round to the back of the building, where steep steps led up to the chalet above.

Syrie showed the necessary appreciation and approval as they were shown around, and then while Blaine tipped the porter a moment later, she went out to the wooden-railed balcony.

There were several lamp-lit fishing vessels in the lagoon, and she could hear the fishermen calling to one another. The air was warm and languid and she felt pleasantly relaxed after the scenic drive from one part of the island to another.

The thought that she and Blaine would possibly make love in her chalet created a feeling which was so intense she could hardly breathe properly, and she realised that for the first time in her life she was ready for that love-making. She also realised just why she had kept making excuses to Craig, and wondered what would have actually transpired on their wedding night. How could I have been swept along like that? she asked herself.

Blaine came out to where she was standing, put his hands on her shoulders and turned her round to face him.

'I think, Syrie Knight, the time has come for us to start enjoying ourselves, don't you?' His voice was soft. 'And there's *one* person I'd like you to forget— at least while we're here.'

Her expression was carefully guarded. 'What are you trying to say?'

'You know what I'm saying. Another thing, *he's* probably enjoying *himself*, right this minute.'

The truth was, she believed him. She hadn't heard from Craig again.

'*This* is what you brought me here for, isn't it?' She sounded angry, but if only he knew how treacherous she was being—for it was what she wanted too.

'Let's get one thing straight. I'm in love with you. I didn't bring you here to act like some tramp. My suggestion to come here wasn't, believe it or not, motivated by lust.'

'What was it motivated by, Blaine?'

'You might say I am negotiating a takeover.'

'A takeover?' Her little laugh was bitter. 'That's priceless.'

'Why is it priceless?'

'I've never belonged to Craig.'

'Well, then?'

Before she quite realised what was happening, he had scooped her into his arms and was carrying her into the main room. He let her down on the floor and she watched him as he removed the linen jacket he was wearing and tossed it over a nearby wicker chair. He then began to unbutton his shirt.

'Blaine—don't try to get to work on me,' she said. Suddenly she meant it, and made to move away from him but he caught her wrist.

'Don't run away. You know you don't want to. Come here.' He looked dynamic and dangerous as he framed her face with his hands and then kissed her, teasing the outline of her lips and savouring their softness. She wanted to protest again, but the protest ended in a shuddering sigh and she kissed him back.

With deliberate gentleness he began to undress her and lowered his lips to her breasts as he discarded each garment.

Later, when she was undressed, she thought he was like a bronze statue—or like a gladiator in Ancient Roman days. She kissed the brown aureoles of his nipples and then looked up at him.

'You're like Michelangelo's David, Blaine.'

He laughed. 'Am I?'

'Yes—or someone who drove a chariot in Ancient Rome. Actually, you're beautiful—in a strong, masculine way, of course.'

'I like to hear these things,' he answered, sounding amused. 'Keep on. But first, say you love me.'

'I love you.'

'You do?'

'Uh-huh.' She laughed shyly.

He began to caress her again, and her arms encircled his neck and then went to his dark blond hair. For a few moments they stood locked together and swaying slightly.

A knock at the door caused them to break apart.

'Oh, heavens!' Syrie caught her breath. 'The door—it might not be locked. I can't . . .' She rushed to the bathroom and then draped a big towel about herself.

A few moments later, Blaine called out, 'You can come out now. The coast's clear.' She could hear the amusement in his voice.

With its wicker and cane furniture and heavy-based reading lamps, the spacious room had a glamorous look, and her green eyes went immediately to the new addition to the décor—a large blue and white jug, which was filled with white daisies.

Blaine was saying, 'I see you've noticed the cause of the untimely interruption. I ordered flowers and they have only just arrived.'

'Thank you, but why *daisies*?' Her voice was brittle.

'The management said they'd do what they could. You don't sound very impressed.' He sounded put-out. 'How was I to know they'd be daisies?'

Her eyes flickered over him. Obviously he had got into his clothes very quickly and his shirt hung open.

I don't know whether I'd be doing the right thing by going to bed with him, she thought. What will he really think of me—*after tonight*?

'Blaine, you're making a mountain out of a molehill,' she told him, before going out to the balcony.

He followed her. 'What is this all about, Syrie? Aren't daisies good enough for a glamorous globetrotter?'

'Now, don't *you* start that!' She swung round. 'What's so unusual about a person visiting other countries? In any case, about the daisies—it's not that.'

'Well, what is it?'

'It's just that daisies have a habit of bringing back unsettling memories of a certain time in my life.'

'I see. Are you referring to your—parents? England, maybe? If so, I'm sorry.'

She opened her mouth to tell him, but she found she couldn't talk about the daisies in Craig's chalet—not now anyway—and so she took a deep breath and said nothing.

'Would you like me to ring reception and have them removed?' Blaine asked.

'Oh, *no*. Not that, Blaine. I'm sorry, really. They're lovely—it's just *me*. Please leave them.'

'Are you sure?' He was eager to please her.

'Positive. By the way, don't you think we'd better begin to think of dressing for dinner? I'd love a bath, actually—or a shower.'

He seemed to sense that her mood towards having him make love to her had changed. 'Fine.' His eyes held hers. 'I'll come back later.'

He came over to her and kissed her lightly.

'Are you OK?'

'Yes, of course.' She smiled. 'I'm sorry if I sounded "switched off".'

After he had gone downstairs, she looked around. The big blue and white jug, filled with the white daisies, stood on the small cane bar, which could also be used for breakfasts and snacks. Next to it was a silver ice-bucket which held a green, silver and white wrapped bottle of champage—ordered, no doubt, by Blaine. For afterwards? As they lay naked in bed together?

Feeling strung up now, she gathered her things together and went through to the bathroom. She washed her hair, styling it later by using the hairdryer which she had brought along with her.

Her bath and toilette complete, she began to dress, taking her time, for it was still early.

She had decided on the slim-fitting white skirt, with double-scooped tier, and shirt to match, before she'd left Blaine's house. White, she knew, did wonderful things to her tan, green eyes and tawny hair. Beneath the skirt she wore a straight slip which ended in a frothy frill.

She slipped her feet into olive-green woven sandals with high heels. Chunky gold ear-rings and a gold bracelet, which had cost her a furtune to buy while she was working in Paris, made a fashion statement which could not be ignored. She knew she looked casually but oh, so expensively beautiful. Outwardly she was the girl she used to be. Inwardly, was another matter.

She unlocked the door so that when Blaine arrived he could knock and walk in, and then she went out to the balcony. A few minutes later, she heard him enter the chalet.

'I hope you don't mind—I just walked in,' he said.

'I left the door unlocked for you to do just that.' He looked so handsome, she thought.

Coming over to her, he took her wrist and drew her up beside him.

'You look stunning—but then, you always do.'

'Thank you.' She smiled. 'I *tried*—for you.'

Unexpectedly, she found that she was touching his hard thighs with her own, and this sent something like a blast of TNT exploding right through her. Moving away from him, she thought it best to go into the main room for her purse, which matched the sandals she was wearing.

He followed her. 'Don't worry, I wasn't going to muss up this perfection.' His blue eyes went to her ear rings and bracelet. 'Very attractive,' he said.

'Well, they should be. Buying them was a personal indulgence on my part.' She laughed a little, still feeling awkward with him now that she had allowed him to undress her a little while ago.

He leaned over and kissed her forehead. 'Well, shall we go?'

'Yes, I think so.' She took a quick breath and looked round the room. 'I'll just leave the lamps burning.'

The chalet they had been invited to was air-conditioned, and it was obvious, even at night, that the views across the sea lagoon and ocean beyond the reef were magnificent.

The cocktail party was being held in a kind of studio upstairs. Taking a cocktail from a waiter's tray, Syrie surveyed the room with interested eyes.

It was an exciting space, with salmon-pink walls, white, thickly woven curtains and cane sofas and wicker peacock chairs, all vividly upholstered. The ceiling was thatched and the colour of a copper coin, and there was sufficient room for people to stand about, particularly in the centre of the room. In fact, it was a room that seemed to have been created for people to stand around in groups, talking—or overlapping to the spacious balcony. There was a bar at one end, and the whole set-up was an exciting backdrop to softly played *sega* music and to guests of all nationalities.

She glanced at Blaine. What was he thinking? she wondered? As he listened to the *sega* music, was he reminded of his scathing remark about Greek bouzouki music?

White-clad staff circulated among guests, proffering trays of island cocktails and snacks; such as samosas—little envelopes of pastry, filled with spiced meat and vegetables—chilibites and other tasty morsels.

As they had presented their invitation card, Syrie had been aware that several women had turned to look at Blaine. Well, he was certainly something to look at, she thought. He projected sexy looks, physical fitness and self-assurance. She found herself thinking now about her reaction when his thighs had touched hers, and shivered slightly.

He broke into her thoughts. 'What are you thinking about so seriously?'

She laughed. 'You're always asking me that question.'
Taking a little sip of her cocktail she went on, 'Actually,
you won't believe me, but I was thinking about
trinitrotoluene.'

His blue eyes narrowed slightly. 'And what makes you
think of high explosives at a time like this? Are you
thinking of blowing up the place?'

'I'll be blowing myself to smithereens if I'm not very
careful,' she answered.

Although they were among so many guests, they were
not yet involved with anyone else.

Blaine's voice was mocking. 'There's nothing to
prevent you.'

'Since he's gone away, you mean? I thought you
didn't want to talk about him?'

They were caught up in a moment where *sega* music
and other people could not intrude.

'I don't. He's always there, though, isn't he? You
make sure of that by always defending him.'

Syrie only half protested as he took her glass and
placed it, along with his own, on a passing tray. He took
two fresh daiquiris and handed her one. His eyes held
hers, challenging her to say something.

'You're often so nasty to me, Blaine. Why?'

'Because I want to hurt you, I guess.'

'But—*why*?'

'Because you keep harping about him, when you've
known from the beginning how it is with us.'

'But you're the one who's harping now. In a
roundabout manner, you always introduce his name.'

They suddenly found themselves scooped up in a
group of people. A dark girl, her hair arranged in a
gleaming chignon—low on the neck and pierced with a
gold pin—and wearing a crimson and gold sari, had
cornered Blaine.

Syrie found herself talking to a dark man who immediately began to go into detail about why it was on the cards that Mauritius was in for another cyclone in the very near future.

'I hope I'm not here then,' she laughed, 'but I thought most cyclones pass Mauritius by?'

'True,' he answered. 'It is not often she gets a severe one—but a big one is on the cards—a violent one which will be long remembered for the havoc it will cause.'

'Well, I hope you're wrong, *monsieur*.' She smiled and glanced over at Blaine. Across the room, their eyes locked, and then she watched him as he excused himself from the sari-clad girl and made his way over to where she was standing with the man who was now talking about the cyclone which had hit Mauritius in April, 1892, and which was reputed to be still the worst in the island's history.

'It killed one thousand two hundred and sixty people,' he was saying. 'That's a lot of people—in any language.'

Blaine placed an arm about Syrie's waist and drew her close to him, and she thrilled to his touch.

'Save me from this man,' she whispered.

'Do you realise how much I've wanted to? I've missed you.'

'What am I supposed to do? Swoon?' She laughed lightly. Turning to her dark companion she said, 'Do excuse me *monsieur*, I think I'd like to choose something deliciously savoury to eat. I have so enjoyed our conversation.'

'Maybe again?' He lifted his glass.

'Yes, of course.'

The cocktail party was warming up and people were beginning to mingle and to introduce themselves. Apparently, they had all arrived on the same day. Once more Syrie found herself separated from Blaine, but her eyes kept searching him out. Once, from across the room, he lifted his glass and toasted her; smiling, she toasted him back. She realised she was getting just a little tipsy.

Later, he managed to get back to her.

'Blaine, do you know what?' She giggled.

His eyes were on her mouth. 'No—what? Tell me.'

'I think I've had too many castor-sugar-coated-frosted-glass daiquiri cocktails. How did it happen? I thought I was being *very* cautious.'

Laughing outright, he said. '*You*—cautious?'

Thinking about how she had been far too cautious to go to bed with Craig, she said, 'I am more cautious than you will ever know.'

People were beginning to leave the party.

'What about dinner?' Blaine asked. 'Are you hungry?'

'I'm so hungry I could crunch half the coral off the reef.'

Hugging her close, he kissed her. 'Come along, then.'

For a moment she clung to him and felt the molten heat of sexy things to come.

They dined in an exciting area of pink-clothed tables. The cocktails, followed by wine, were still going to work on Syrie.

'You look radiant.' Blaine reached for her hand. 'Are you pleased we came?'

'I'm pleased, but I shouldn't be, of course.' Suddenly, she began to feel aggressive towards Blaine and the male species in general.

'Why?' His eyes were frankly curious.

'You know why, as well as I do. I'm going to end up in bed with you. That's right, isn't it? It's on the cards, just as—according to the man I was speaking to—Mauritius is in for another cyclone in the very near future. What is more, you can't blame it on bouzouki music.' As an afterthought she added, 'Of course, there *was* the sega music.'

'What's all this about, Syrie?'

'At least, though, the daisies were for *me*. They had nothing to do with Hélène.' She wanted to keep on at him.

'What's Hélène's name being dragged into this for? I think you've become aggressively tight, Syrie.' Blaine's eyes appeared almost black at this moment.

She held his angry gaze and then dropped her lashes. 'You expected me to share your bed tonight, didn't you? Right from the start. "Pack an overnight bag," you said. "This is strictly on the level." Hah!'

'If you deem it necessary to ask, it means that you want to end up in bed—in fact, if it hadn't been for the bloody daisies, that is where you would have ended up and would, most probably, still be there. Do you *want* to end up there?'

'I did, but I'm not sure now.' She held up her glass and stared at the golden wine, and when she put the glass to her lips, Blaine reached out and took it from her and put it to one side. 'Enough of that! I should have noticed for myself—you've had too much.'

'If I have, it's thanks to you.' She wanted to *fight* with him. 'To get back to our conversation—I . . .'

He cut in, 'You've obviously been giving it some thought—even before we came here. That's right, isn't it?'

'I've been giving a whole lot of thought, actually, and not just tonight, either. For some time.'

'Why is this, Syrie?'

All about them there was the constant buzz of conversation.

'I—think I'm in love with you,' she said, very softly. 'But, after what I've been through . . .'

'After what you've put yourself through, is more to the point.'

'I'm afraid of falling in love again.' She began fidgeting with her gold bracelet.

'You were never really in love with Craig.'

'I don't know if I'm ready, after all, for this—with you, Blaine.'

'The only way you'll find out is if I move in, upstairs, with you. Right?'

'I don't think I want to.' She drew a deep breath.

'You're a bundle of contradictions,' he said angrily.

'What is so amazing is that *I never used to be*!' She lifted her voice.

'Don't expect to have my undivided attention while you're trying to make up your mind. Oh, come on, let's dance.' He got up and came round for her.

On the dance-floor, she leaned against him, wanting him as she knew he wanted her. Feeling a growing need to have him kiss her, she tilted her face towards him, but he went on holding her lightly, his hands loosely linked at the base of her spine.

'Don't try that on me until you're very, very sure,' he said. 'I'm in love with you, but I don't want you like this. You don't owe me anything for bringing you here.'

'You say you're in love with me, but you don't want me *like this*. What do you mean?' she asked, in a hard little voice. 'What are you talking about?'

'I'm talking about your loyalty to Craig Knox and your uncertainty when it comes to me. However, I've reached the stage where I've had it! If you want to go on waiting to see what he is going to come up with— so be it.'

'What you don't understand, Blaine, is that I have found the glimpses of Craig's character quite revolting. Can't you understand how cheapened I feel?'

'Put it down to experience,' he answered quite brutally.

'Experience only relegates a woman to the scrap-heap, Mr Cartwright. I take that remark as an insult.'

'Take it as you like.' He sounded almost bored.

The music ended and they went back to their table.

As they sat down he said, 'You'd try the patience of a saint. Do you know that, Syrie? When are you going to reach saturation point?'

She stood up. 'I'm going to my chalet.'

'Fine.' He swirled the contents of his glass, and then, after drinking what was left, he stood up and came round to her.

As they walked towards the A-framed double-storey building in which they were accommodated, he said, 'I'll see you to the door.'

'Thank you. These steps at the back of the building do give me the creeps, as it so happens.' Her voice was like ice.

'Are you going to be nervous up here on your own? Would you like to swap? If you take my chalet, you'll have neighbours right next door—not just beneath you.'

'I'm not the nervous type. It's just these steep stairs at the back.' They had reached the top, and she waited for him to unlock her coral-coloured door.

When they were inside he said, 'I'm aware of the conflict which has been tearing you apart, Syrie. Can't you accept that it's over? Craig's gone and you don't owe him a second thought. When I said I was negotiating a takeover—I meant just that. In fact, I've got Robert French, who handles matters for Design Dimension, making investigations. I am determined to trace Craig—for one thing, he owes my company a lot of money, and for another, I want you to get him out of your system. You'll probably discover that he . . .'

'I don't want to hear about it,' she cut in.

'Well, you're just damn well *going* to hear about it! Don't be so childish! Jurrah, for what it's worth, is also making his own investigations. He came to see me, actually, to find out whether I had anything—anything at all—which might assist him. Craig's work references from Australia were in the safe. I gave Jurrah permission to photostat them. Perhaps I should have told you, before now . . .'

'*Perhaps*? Perhaps you should have told me? But of course you should have told me. How could you, Blaine? I'm seeing a new side to you. Jurrah is just about the lowest form of life. Do you realise what this could mean? He will show no mercy towards Craig if he finds him.'

'Tell me, does it make you feel good—standing up for Craig? Have you forgotten what he did to you—left you standing . . . He doesn't deserve any mercy. Let's get this straight—I want to marry you and this guy's memory lingers on with you—well, *forget*!' Blaine was furious and his voice had risen.

'Terrific. You're in love with me. You want to marry me, and yet you upset me by allowing an unscrupulous ratty moneylender to help you in your investigations? Do you know how despicable that is? I want to have no part in this. I don't want to see Craig thrown into some gaol.' She began to cry softly. 'I wouldn't like to see *anybody* thrown into gaol—let alone Craig. He does have some good points, you know.'

'Name two!' Blaine answered ruthlessly. 'But let's be practical for a moment. These were merely references. The only things of any interest were the names and addresses of three graphic design studios in Sydney. These firms probably know as little about Craig as we do.'

'Just get out of here,' Syrie told him. Was all this to get out of having him make love to her? she asked herself.

Blaine's fury broke then. He was half-way to the door when he said, 'I'll be wanting to leave this place about eight tomorrow. 'We'll leave after breakfast . . .'

'If I can *face* breakfast,' she flung back at him.

'OK—if you can face breakfast—but—be on time, regardless.'

'By the way,' she went on, 'I'm going to resign. I don't want to work for you, Blaine.'

'Fine. Resignation accepted.'

'And I'm moving out of your house.' As she spoke, she felt she had suddenly lost complete control of her life.

'In that case, I'll help you to pack,' he called out brutally as he slammed the door.

After he'd gone she wept on the balcony.

The lanterns on the fishing-boats reflected pure, shivering gold in the still black waters of the lagoon.

CHAPTER TEN

ALTHOUGH she had been up since the flush of dawn, Syrie, according to Blaine's instructions of the night before, was ten minutes late for breakfast.

He was sitting at a pink-clothed table, and as he glanced up she sensed his smouldering resentment.

In turn, she greeted him with hostility.

'I know I'm ten minutes late, Blaine. I know you said eight o'clock, but just don't go on about it.'

'As you so aptly express it—let's just get going and order breakfast and get it over.' His voice was hard. Obviously, she thought, feeling sick, he had lost his personal interest in her.

To avoid drawing attention to herself, she sat down.

'I'm not hungry,' she said.

'Well, I am. I'm very hungry,' he answered callously.

Her eyes went to the basket of exotic island fruit and croissants which a waiter had just placed on the table.

At Blaine's request, the waiter lifted a bottle of champagne from an ice-bucket and began to mix mimosas; one for her and one for Blaine.

Another waiter came and presented them with menus, and Syrie shook her head. 'Not for me, thank you. I'll just have *café au lait*.'

'Ah, but *mademoiselle*—nothing? You are sure?'

Her eyes went to the warm, flaky croissants.

'Maybe just a croissant, thank you.' She smiled up at him.

When they were alone, Blaine said, 'Since I was up at

five, I had a swim. Did you want to swim before we left?'
He glanced carelessly at the simple white dress she was
wearing, which was nipped in at the waist by a narrow
suede belt. Around her neck she had tied a flimsy green
scarf, which drew attention to her eyes. Her long, tanned
legs ended in beige high-heeled sandals. She looked cool
and lovely, but the tension showed in her face.

'*I* got carried away.' She looked at him resentfully. *I*
was up for most of the night, but I wasn't in the mood for
a swim this morning—*unlike you*.'

'Well, I guess that's your problem.' Leisurely, he slipped
down on his chair and leaned his shoulders against the back
of it. His blue eyes narrowed. 'It's entirely up to you what
you do, and that goes for everything. In other words, if you
want to on shielding Craig and feeling some sort of useless
guilt—so be it, but don't expect me to sit back and do
nothing about it. You've also got this ridiculous sense of
guilt about his possessions. I couldn't care less about them,
but if you want to go shuffling them from one shop
outbuilding to another, in an effort to save them from
being reclaimed, that's also your affair. I feel sorry for you,
actually. You're a fool.'

'Thank you.' Her voice was brittle.

'You're welcome.'

After a moment, trying to hold on to her temper and to
sound reasonable she said, 'It's just that I can't help
feeling sorry for him. He doesn't deserve all the things
which you've said about him. After all, I got to know him
quite well.'

Blaine laughed at this, but she was determined to have
her say.

'You've played right into Jurrah's hands and, to use an
expression of yours and Craig's, he's out to nail Craig.
That's so, isn't it?'

'Yes, that is so—and so am I. I've already told you that.'

She went on, 'Once Jurrah's tracked Craig down, he'll stop at nothing. You cold-bloodedly gave Jurrah something to work on—something to go on. Surely you could have just worked along your own lines—with this Robert French, if you'd wanted to?'

'Go on, Syrie. You interest me, you really do, from a psychological point of view, that is.'

Angrily, she watched him as he began to eat the food which had now been placed before him, and then, unable to stand it another moment, she turned to look at the sea.

It was all so wasted, she thought bitterly. The palms, hibiscus, bougainvillaea, creamy-white sand and the dusky-pink sunbeds, draped around the sparkling blue pool.

Blaine broke into her thoughts. 'About last night, and the things we said. I want you to go on staying in the house and to go on working to DD.'

'That was hardly the impression you gave me. In fact, you even said you'd help me to pack.'

'Forget what I said. I've got a quick temper and I have discovered that goes for you, too. You should know about my temper by now.' He straightened up and reached across the table for her hand which was on the pink cloth.

She took a long breath. 'Sometimes I can't believe all this is really happening—or, should I say—has really happened.'

'Well, it has happened and I intend to see the latter part through—that is, I intend to get our relationship underway.'

'Seeing the first part through, though, means seeing Craig punished. And if I know you at all, severely punished—going to gaol.'

'How do you know? You're the only one who is harping on gaol. I want him to pay back the money he helped himself to—even if it takes a hundred years.'

Tanned and lean, he was wearing denim jeans which were tight across his hips. His denim shirt was open, and she saw that he'd tossed a light denim jacket over a nearby chair.

Looking at her again he said, 'I'm trying to figure you out—and failing dismally, I might add. Why—*just why*—are you so intent in sticking up for this guy? You go on trying to prove that in some cases he has actually been framed, and yet you have stated that he has cheapened you.'

He reached into the ice-bucket for the champagne, but when he made to mix her another mimosa—peach juice with champagne, she covered her glass with the palm of her hand and shook her head.

'No, thank you. I'm not in the mood for a champagne breakfast.'

Suddenly, he got up and came round to her chair and, regardless of the other guests who were also having a casual breakfast on the terrace, he placed his cheek against hers and then he kissed her.

'Let's stop all this nonsense. Are you ready? Maybe we'll come back here another time—when we're both ready for it—not that I wasn't ready last night.' He gave her a disarming smile.

She took an unsettled little breath. 'And so, Blaine, we'll be *right* back where we started? I go on living in your house until my chalet becomes vacant—for I fully intend to move into it—and I continue to go on working for Design Dimension? In other words, forget about the fact that you gave Jurrah important information.'

'Oh, for Pete's sake!' Blaine began to walk on ahead.

On the drive back, Syrie brooded on the fact that she had lost touch with so many friends and relatives in England. On the other hand, however, she was thankful that she *had* maintained such a slack correspondence with a few of them. As a result, not many people would know about her disastrous romance. She saw no urgency, at this stage, anyway, in informing any of them.

The following weeks were busy and she was doing more and more in the studio. She had offered to help with fashion shots, and Blaine was satisfied since, he'd said, she'd had experience in Paris. He'd resorted to mockery, but admitted later that her help had been invaluable.

She was also involved in an audio-visual presentation, and the entire staff of Design Dimension had worked until two in the morning to meet the deadline, while the rain had pelted down and battered the old plantation mansion. She found herself wondering whether the dark man at Trou aux Biches had been right about a cyclone on the way.

Testing and sorting slides to music and narration was exhausting work. There were slides of girls wearing wide-brimmed hats; girls at poolsides; girls on huge peacock-throne chairs; girls at farm gates . . . The noise of the blowing fan had nearly driven Syrie mad, not to mention Andy's voice, droning on and on.

'What's the last command you have, Blaine? OK— 4D1 . . .'

Things went wrong with the computer and they'd had to start all over again.

Liselle stayed up to help and brought trays of things to eat and tea, coffee and juices to drink. Eventually the presentation was complete. Syrie felt a spasm of regret, for she would have more time on her hands to brood on the fact that Craig had callously left her with debts which had nothing to do with her, but since he had used the account in her name—and got away with it—she was still trying to pay that off.

Blaine was unaware of the bitterness she was feeling towards Craig.

'What do you think of this slide?' he asked, several nights later when she was helping him in the studio.

Feeling strung-up beyond words, she made no attempt to hide her feelings.

'It's too green,' she answered irritably.

He looked amused. 'You're coming on. So, you think it's too green?'

'That's what I said. In fact, I know it's too green, Blaine. You can't possibly use it. Throw it in the basket.'

To her surprise, he removed the slide from the circular tray and dropped it into the basket.

He looked at her again. 'Do you mind working at night like this?'

'I offered, didn't I? You didn't force me to work tonight. Look, can we just get on with this, Blaine, and forget about my personal feelings?'

He was angry now. 'Don't take your bad temper out on me. I had nothing to do with your big romance of the year.'

'Don't keep calling it that! Either it's the romance of the twentieth century, or it's the big romance of the year. I'm sick and tired of it.'

'Oh, go to bed, Syrie.' He stood up and went towards the open french doors. 'You're beginning to bore me,' he said, almost beneath his breath.

Leaving him, she called out, 'Well, it won't be for long. I'll be moving out soon. Won't you be pleased?'

Jubala Jurrah phoned her the next morning, and every muscle in her body seemed to go into a spasm at the sound of that detestable voice.

'I have some news for you, *mademoiselle*. Will you come in and see me? My secretary will make the necessary appointment. What time suits you?'

Glancing at the small battery-operated clock on her desk, she said, 'Twelve o'clock.'

'Well, I'll put you through to my secretary and she will make a note of that.'

'Before you go, Monsieur Jurrah, is it good—or bad?'

There was a pause and then he said, 'It depends by what you mean—good or bad—but you are not going to like it. That is all I am prepared to say at the moment.' The line clicked and then his secretary's voice asked Syrie what she could do for her.

The drive to Port Louis seemed endless, with one bullock cart after another blocking her way, and she swore as she waited for a chance to overtake them on the narrow roads between green and gold cane fields. Once, she had to swerve to miss an ancient woman who suddenly appeared from nowwhere, her purple and silver sari flapping around her frail body.

Blaine had shown no surprise when Syrie had told him she was going into Port Louis to follow up a prospective client, and she had come as she was, wearing a white blouse with a cross-over bodice and frilled collar, and trousers with a hessian belt.

After she had parked the car, she almost ran towards the steps which led into the shabby house, and she caught the heel of one woven sandal in a crack in the tarmac and wrenched her foot. Stopping in her tracks, and standing quite still until the pain had subsided slightly, she felt the warm heat of tears in her eyes.

Directly she was shown into Jubala Jurrah's dingy office, he stood up and came round to the chair she had occupied on her first visit, and held it out for her.

'Please, sit down, *mademoiselle.*'

Moodily, tensely, she watched him as he went back to his own seat, and when he had settled himself he placed his elbows on his desk and peaked his plump fingers. There was a terrible undercurrent.

'I will get straight to the point,' he said. 'Knox has been

traced to a cattle station in—what do they say?—
the sticks of Australia. That is correct, I think?' He gave
one of his pained half-smiles. He slid a sheet of paper
across his desk and, reluctantly, Syrie reached for it. She
stared down at the paper, seeing nothing. She lifted her
eyes.

'And—so—you've found him?'

'But of course. I explained to you, did I not, that if
anyone was to find this man it would be me?'

'With the kind help of Monsieur Cartwright, *of
course*!' Her voice was bitter. 'What else do you have to
tell me, *monsieur*?' She was so taut now, she thought
she'd snap.

He half closed his eyes and looked at her.

'There is some bad news—and yet—good, as you will
discover for yourself. Craig Knox, my dear young lady,
is already married. He was a married man when he met
you and arranged to marry you.'

The colour drained from Syrie's tanned face, but after
a moment she managed to say, 'I don't understand.
They were divorced, *monsieur*, in New Zealand. This,
he told me himself. Someone has got their wires crossed.
I don't believe this.'

'It is true,' he told her. 'You'd better accept it.'

Oh, dear heaven, I'm going to faint, she thought des-
perately. I was taken in by a married man. I've even
been *paying his debts*. She felt sick.

Jubala Jurrah must have signalled for his secretary to
come through to his office, because Syrie suddenly
found a glass of something between her fingers.

Quite kindly, Jurrah was saying, 'Drink this, young
lady. It can only do you good and it is quite safe, believe
me. I always keep a little something in my office.'

Syrie took several small sips and shuddered helplessly.

'Are you all right?' Jurrah asked.

She swallowed again. 'Yes. Yes, thank you. It's just been a shock.'

Jurrah went on, 'Before Knox's wife left him, she had expressed her intention of divorcing him. They then lost touch, as sometimes happens, and after a period of time had elapsed *he* was *genuinely* of the opinion that this was what she had done. He thus believed himself to be free to marry you. Small consolation, I am aware. It seems to be a trait of Knox to conduct his affairs carelessly.'

'Has he gone back to her?'

'No. I have a complete report. I realise you are finding this news shocking, since you appear to be a fastidious young lady.' His smile was like a grimace.

'The very *thought* of—bigamy—is shocking, Monsieur Jurrah.' Her voice was dangerously calm and quiet. 'This, along with learning of the death of my parents, is one of the worst moments of my life. I feel degraded, to say the least.'

'But you have had a lucky escape, *mademoiselle*. That is the good news. Everything has worked out in your case for the best.'

Craig? Not Craig, surely? Syrie drove back into the centre of Port Louis, parked the car and sat staring through the windscreen. Feeling completely unreal, she got out of the car and then walked around the town aimlessly. Misery seeks misery, and she found herself in those places which were shabby, dilapidated and grimy; jostled on the narrow litter-strewn pavements, she ignored the more exciting areas, which were vibrant with colour.

Hours later she got back into the car, after having to search for it because she had forgotten where she had parked it, and drove back to the coast.

As she entered Blaine's mansion, he came into the hall to meet her.

'Where the hell have you been?' He grasped her shoulders. 'I've been out of my mind about you. I had a phone call from Jurrah explaining the position, and he ended up by telling me that you'd been in and had just left. When you didn't arrive back, I drove to Port Louis to look for you.'

'I don't want to talk, right now, and, after all I've been through today, I badly need a bath.'

She tried to brush past him, but he caught her to him.

'I don't want to see you looking like this, Syrie. Nothing matters to me—but you. And after all, you didn't go through with the—marriage.'

'No, I escaped by the skin of my hairy chin-chin. Aren't I lucky? Do you realise how cheap I feel—paying his debts and all? Well, you'll get your money back, I suppose, in the long run. That's what you *all* wanted, isn't it? To see justice. To see him flung into a filthy gaol. Craig's not gaol material. Can't you see *that*?'

'To hell with the money. I love you, Syrie.'

'If you do, I don't want to hear about it. I don't want to know about it.' She was almost shouting. 'Just leave me alone. The lot of you!'

'Listen to me, darling . . .'

'No. I never want to listen to another man again in my whole life. I'm going away. Let's face it,' she took a gulp of air, 'I always run away when I'm shattered. I want to be by myself.'

'I'm going with you,' Blaine said. 'Wherever you want to go, darling.'

'No. Just leave me alone, Blaine.'

Suddenly Blaine's fury broke. 'I could kill that bastard,' he said. 'I love you. You're very dear to me. The fact that Craig had a—some sort of place—in your life is inconsequential to me—except the harm which he has done to you.'

Three days later, she flew to the island of red lateritic
soil and rock—which was once a part of Southern Africa.
The island of Madagascar was supposed to be still on the
move; a few millimetres a year, in fact.

She landed at Antananarivo at sunset, went through the
checks at the airport and was driven by a taxi which
awaited her, along pot-holed roads towards the city which
glimmered like dark gold.

As she was shown to her room at the Hilton Hotel, she
realised that she was once again in a strange part of the
world—where time seemed to stand still, according to
some people.

Am I doomed to run away and lick my wounds? she
asked herself as she listened to the language around her,
which was strange, and vaguely, she imagined,
Polynesian. On the way to the hotel, she had noticed that
the architecture was strange and different. During the day
time there would be flowers in market-places, fruit and
vegetables banked high, and stalls of attractive basket-
ware, leatherware, vivid fabrics, herbs and piles of spices;
but she was not here to sightsee. She was here to 'cleanse
herself' of Craig Knox and a man called Jubala Jurrah.

In the morning she flew to Tamatave, capital of the
East Coast and a major port of Madagascar. Glimpses of
the city revealed wide boulevards and grand, if faded,
villas. The waters of the Indian Ocean were warm and
they lapped at wonderfully white beaches, which were
fringed by filaos trees.

Pointing to the rickshaws, when she was on the way to
catch her flight to Ste Marie Island, her driver said,
'*Pousse-pousse.*' She smiled and did her best to appear
excited and thrilled with everything, which she would
have been, under different circumstances. Why couldn't
she have been with Blaine? she thought. Blaine—from the
beginning.

It was hot and humid and her clothes began to stick to her body; she longed to reach her destination.

Her nerves were taut as she boarded an Air Madagascar prop-jet on her way from Tamatave to Ste Marie Island, some thirty minutes away, and which could have been likened to a splinter in the Indian Ocean.

The short flight was uneventful and she landed on the tropical island where, indeed, time did seem to be standing quite still. It was all so beautiful, but she was only capable of feeling miserable.

Her hotel, which was on the northern tip of Ile Ste Marie, was reached by boat, and it was another dream-world. It consisted of comfortable, palm-frond huts, a tiny bar and an outdoor restaurant. *Pirogues*—long narrow canoes, made from a single tree trunk—lay on the white beach, and coco palms curved over the water, which stretched—turquoise-blue—into the misty distance.

In the days to come, she gave vent to her feelings in the privacy of her little hut, and on several occasions she wept. She wept for the parents she'd lost, she wept because she wanted Blaine and missed him and some-times she wept for nothing.

Blaine, she realised, must have been bitterly hurt when she'd left secretly. In a note she'd written: 'I'll be back. I promise. Besides, all my things are here. Right? Syrie from Athens.'

After two weeks, she began to feel starving again. Light-heartedly, she learned to eat fresh heart of palm and tiny clams—called *tek-tek*, from the sand at the edge of the water; not to mention crayfish, which she'd always loved.

Ironically, after what she'd said about *men*, her constant companion was an elderly man who reminded her of a Greek tycoon, which was not surprising since, he'd told her, his mother had been a Greek. His name was Christakis Marino, and he was writing a novel, and she had offered to do some typing for him.

With Christakis, she felt safe to confide in him; more so, in fact, than she would have confided in her own father, she supposed. She felt safe to drink with him and was introduced to the local Malagasy wine and Three Horses beer.

She found herself saying, '*Manahona atopoko*,' instead of 'How are you?' and '*Tsara famisoatra*,' instead of 'Fine, thank you.' What was more, she was beginning to feel just that. Fine.

On the day that Blaine arrived, she was spread out on a shocking-pink and blue towel on the white, deserted beach. Her slim body looked like pure copper.

She wasn't aware of him until he spoke her name.

'Syrie?'

Her senses jumped to life and she opened her lovely green eyes and just stared and stared, while the joy which had sprung to life continued to flood every part of her being.

Eventually she was able to say, 'Blaine, what are you *doing* here? Am I seeing things? I can't believe this is happening. How did you know where to find me? Or—didn't you? Is this just a coincidence?'

'What do you think I'm doing here? I've come to take you *home*.' As he spoke, her eyes went over him, and she went on staring at him and then followed his graceful, masculine movements as he bent to kneel down beside her.

He stretched out his arms and gathered her body up to meet his.

'What is more important, right this minute, is—are you pleased to see me?' he said.

'I'm so pleased, I could eat you.' She laughed a little. 'Oh, Blaine, let me feel you next to me. It feels like a lifetime.'

'Don't you *ever* run away from me again, Syrie Knight. I'll never have enough of you. I love you.' He kissed her and then drew back. 'How are you? You're so much more brown. So thin . . . but gorgeously thin.' His exciting blue eyes went to her small breasts, which were barely covered by the bikini top which she was wearing, and then he cupped her nipples beneath the material. 'I'm glad to see that you aren't topless,' he said. 'I'd be wild with jealousy—even if there is no one here at the moment. What have you been doing with yourself?'

'Eating.' She laughed.

His eyes went over her. 'Eating? I don't believe it.'

'It's true. I swim, walk, sleep and sleep and sleep and—oh, I've been doing some typing—for a wonderful man, who looks just like Anthony Quinn. He's been so kind to me. He's a novelist. You'll like him.'

'I won't! You're making me jealous.'

'You needn't be. He's been like a protective father. A few days ago I went with him to Tamatave, where he posted off the first four chapters of his book. His publishers were waiting for them. Then we parted company for an hour or so. He had some private business to attend to. I explored and did a little shopping. I even bought you something—and something wonderful for myself. It's a cotton garment, something like a caftan, actually. It's the colour of jacaranda flowers and I can't tell you how glamorous I feel in it. Now I'm glad I bought it. Now that you're here.'

'I can't wait to see you in it. Tell me about this man, though. I'm still jealous.' Blaine smiled.

'His name is Christakis Marino. As I said, he came here to write a novel. He had a daughter, my age. His daughter and his wife were killed in an air crash over some remote desert. What is so tragic is the fact that he was the pilot. He survived the crash, which is unbelievable.' She broke off and glanced around.

'Where are your things?'

'They were taken to my hut. Like you, I travelled light. You're up on me, though, you even have a caftan the colour of jacaranda flowers.' He spread his hands and looked down at his cotton trousers and the cotton shirt which was hanging open.

At that moment Syrie's pulses quickened, then she looked up and saw Christakis loping towards them. He was tanned and looked the picture of health and strength.

Christakis did not seem surprised to see Blaine, who had got to his feet and was dusting the powdery beach sand from his trousers. Christakis held out a hand, and then Syrie saw the two men exchange glances of appraisal as they shook hands.

'I think this girl is ready to go back now,' Christakis was saying. 'I am glad you have come for her.'

Feeling slightly out of things, Syrie decided to joke. 'If I go back—what about your typing?'

'Ah, do not think I will not be tormented by the fact that I will have to do this myself, Syrie, but that does not mean I do not want to see you fly away to happiness.' Christakis turned to Blaine.

'When she first came here, she did nothing. She ate nothing. She saw nothing—not even me—but eventually the storm was over and I watched it blow out to sea. Soon, she will tell you, I was teaching her to eat fresh heart of palm and *tek-tek* from the sand on the edge of the water. For these favours,' he laughed lightly, 'she has been doing some work on the portable typewriter for me.' His voice was low and gravelly.

Syrie's green eyes were thoughtful as she listened to all this, and then she said 'So, Christakis, what *did* you get up to that day in Tamatave, after we parted company for a while? Some very private business, you said. Come on, now. I'm waiting.'

'I posted four chapters of my manuscript. But you know that, Syrie.' He grinned.

'You also phoned Blaine, didn't you?'

'Surely, Syrie, it is not possible I did the wrong thing by taking matters into my own hands and phoning Mauritius?' His voice was mocking.

Blaine placed an arm about Syrie's shoulders and she looked into his blue eyes. 'I'm not complaining—just asking.'

'OK, then. And now, I will see you both later, huh?' Christakis smiled broadly.

'And—drinks on the house tonight,' Blaine called after him.

Christakis turned. 'We have much to celebrate, huh?'

Blaine scooped Syrie up in his arms and she screamed girlishly and kicked her legs.

'I know where your hut is,' he was saying against her mouth.

On the bed, in her palm-frond hut, she stretched her tall, lovely body against his. Blaine had removed her bikini and thrown off his clothes. She turned to liquid, or so it seemed, before their tanned bodies became tangled. Syrie's body and lips felt exquisitely sensitive to his lips and his hands, and she could think of nothing else but having him close to her.

As love and passion took command, she felt as if she was being lifted up to become part of the very universe, where she seemed to be flying among a luminous band of stars. With them and with Blaine, she encircled the heavens.

Afterwards, they lay spent and breathing quickly.

'I've made enquiries,' he said after a while. 'There's a little church in Tamatave where such matters as having the banns called for three weeks can be discreetly overlooked. We'll fly there tomorrow and our friend Christakis will go along and see us married. We'll come back here and have a party.'

After a moment she said, laughing a little, 'But I've got nothing to wear . . .'

'I've been thinking about that. How about a cotton caftan—the colour of a cluster of jacaranda blossoms—designed and made in Tamatave?' He tickled the corner of her mouth with his tongue. They laughed together and then Blaine went on, 'I've invited Christakis to spend some time with us—when he's ready. He will probably write his next novel there.'

Syrie was suddenly very happy.

'Oh, Blaine . . . I love you. The knowledge that I'd probably never see this man again has caused me endless depression. Christakis has helped to make up for someone I loved very much. My father. I think I've grown to mean something to him, too. In me, he sees a daughter he lost. Thank you, darling. You're so . . .'

'Patient?' Blaine cut in, grinning.

'You're anything but patient,' she laughed, and she found herself thinking—Craig was the patient one, but then, it had suited him to be patient. I'll always know where I stand with this bully, beside me.

'What are you laughing at?' Blaine's voice was soft.

'I'm glad you're not patient. I like you the way you are.'

'Like?' He bent over her.

'*Love*. Do I have to go into such detail, after what has just taken place in this little palm-frond hut on a fragment *just off* a red hump of lateritic soil and rock?' She laughed lightly. 'Darling, I'm so glad it happened here. We must come back to Madagascar again one day.'

'Bring in some more accounts for Design Dimension,' Blaine answered, 'and I'll charter a plane.'

COMING SOON FROM MILLS & BOON!

Your chance to win the fabulous

VAUXHALL ASTRA MERIT 1.2 5-DOOR

Plus

2000 RUNNER UP PRIZES OF WEEKEND BREAKS & CLASSIC LOVE SONGS ON CASSETTE

SEE
♥ MILLS & BOON BOOKS ♥
THROUGHOUT JULY & AUGUST FOR DETAILS!

THE COMPELLING
AND UNFORGETTABLE SAGA OF
THE CALVERT FAMILY

| **April** | **August** | **November** |
| £2.95 | £3.50 | £3.50 |

From the American Civil War to the outbreak of World War I, this sweeping historical romance trilogy depicts three generations of the formidable and captivating Calvert women – Sarah, Elizabeth and Catherine.

The ravages of war, the continued divide of North and South, success and failure, drive them all to discover an inner strength which proves they are true Calverts.

Top author Maura Seger weaves passion, pride, ambition and love into each story, to create a set of magnificent and unforgettable novels.

W❤RLDWIDE